STONE ARCH BOOKS
a capstone imprint

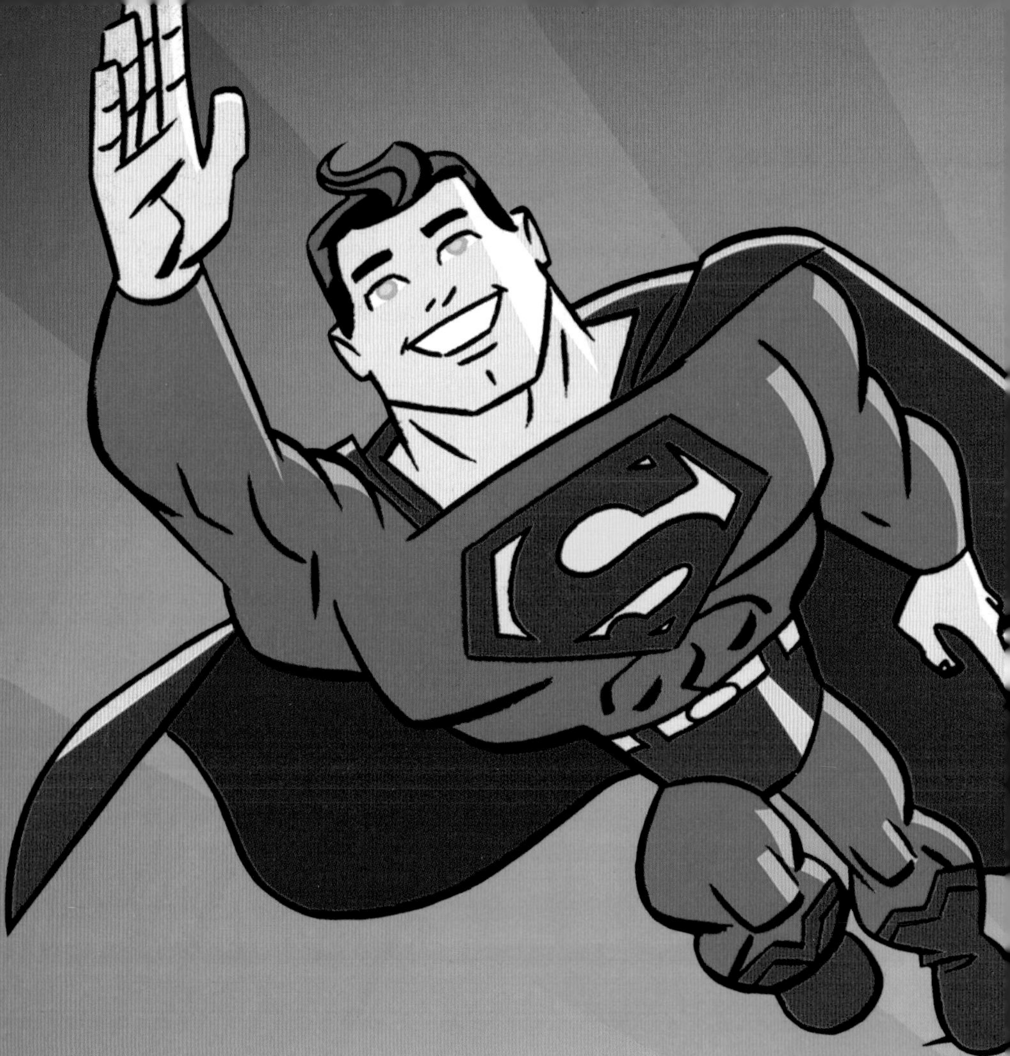

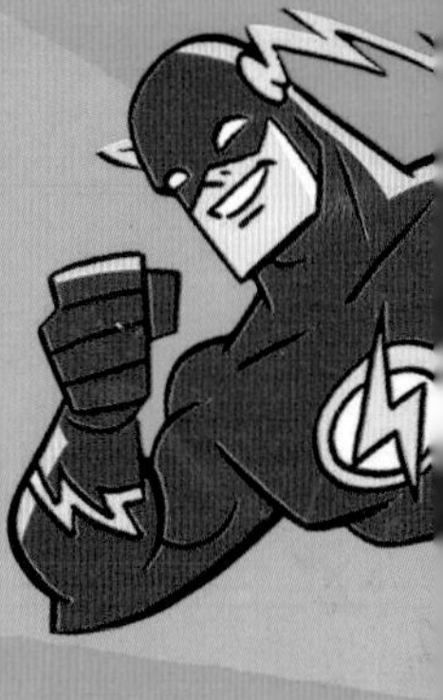

STONE ARCH BOOKS™
Published in 2014
A Capstone Imprint
1710 Roe Crest Drive
North Mankato, MN 56003
www.capstonepub.com

Originally published by DC Comics in the U.S. in single magazine form as DC Super Friends #12.

DC Comics
1700 Broadway, New York, NY 10019
A Warner Bros. Entertainment Company

Cataloging-in-Publication Data is available at the Library of Congress website:
ISBN: 978-1-4342-9225-4 (library binding)

Summary: The Super Friends have never faced a challenge like this before! What will they do when confronted with the menace of Starro and the Pirates? Each library bound book in this action packed series features a comics glossary, visual discussion questions, and writing prompts.

STONE ARCH BOOKS
Ashley C. Andersen Zantop *Publisher*
Michael Dahl *Editorial Director*
Sean Tulien *Editor*
Heather Kindseth *Creative Director*
Brann Garvey and Alison Thiele *Designers*
Kathy McColley *Production Specialist*

DC COMICS
Rachel Gluckstern Original U.S. Editor

Printed in China.
032014 008085LEOF14

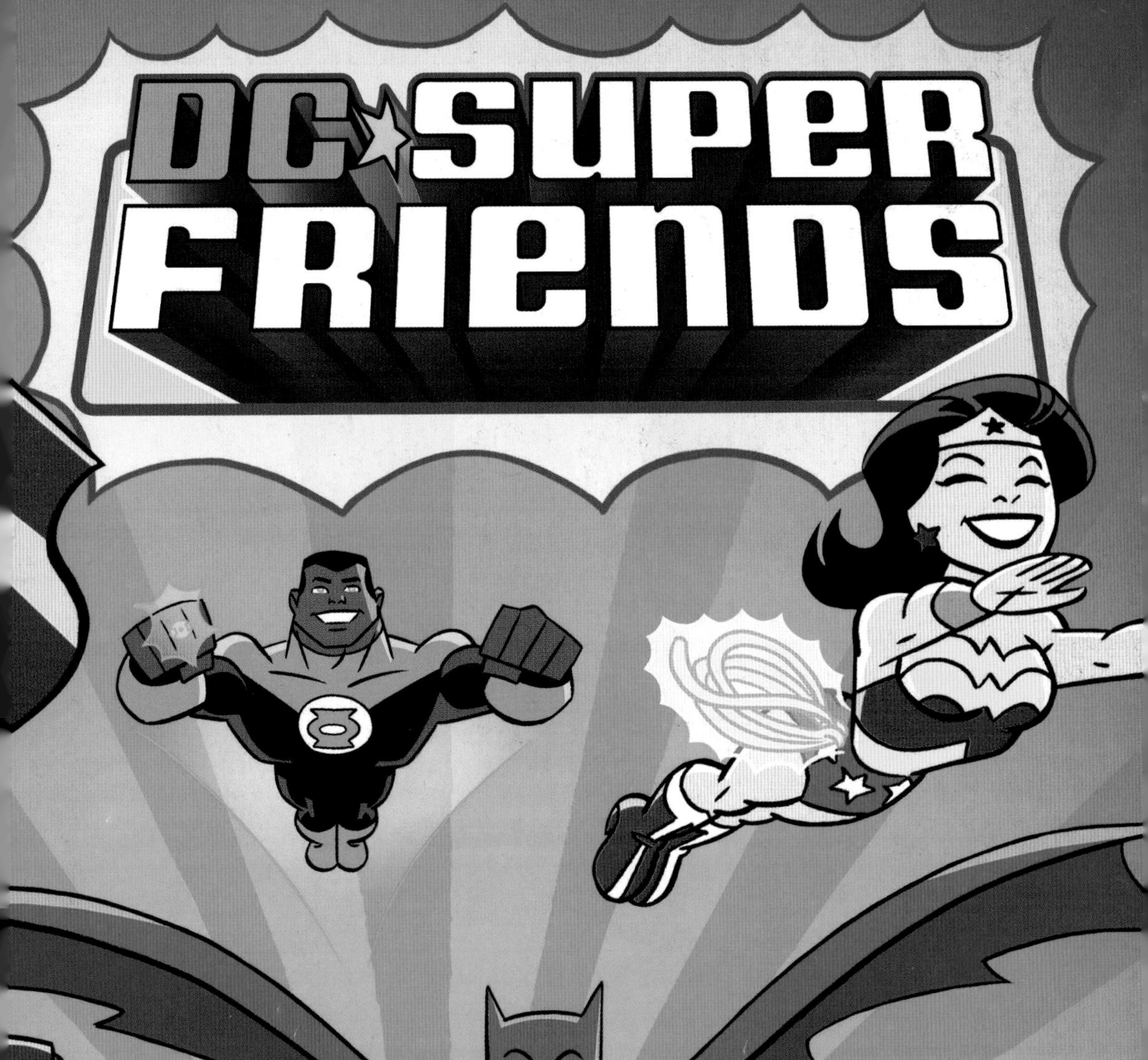
DC SUPER FRIENDS

Starro and the Pirates

Sholly Fisch .... writer
Stewart McKenny .... penciller
Dan Davis .... inker
Heroic Age .... colorist
Travis Lanham.................... letterer
J. Bone .... cover artist

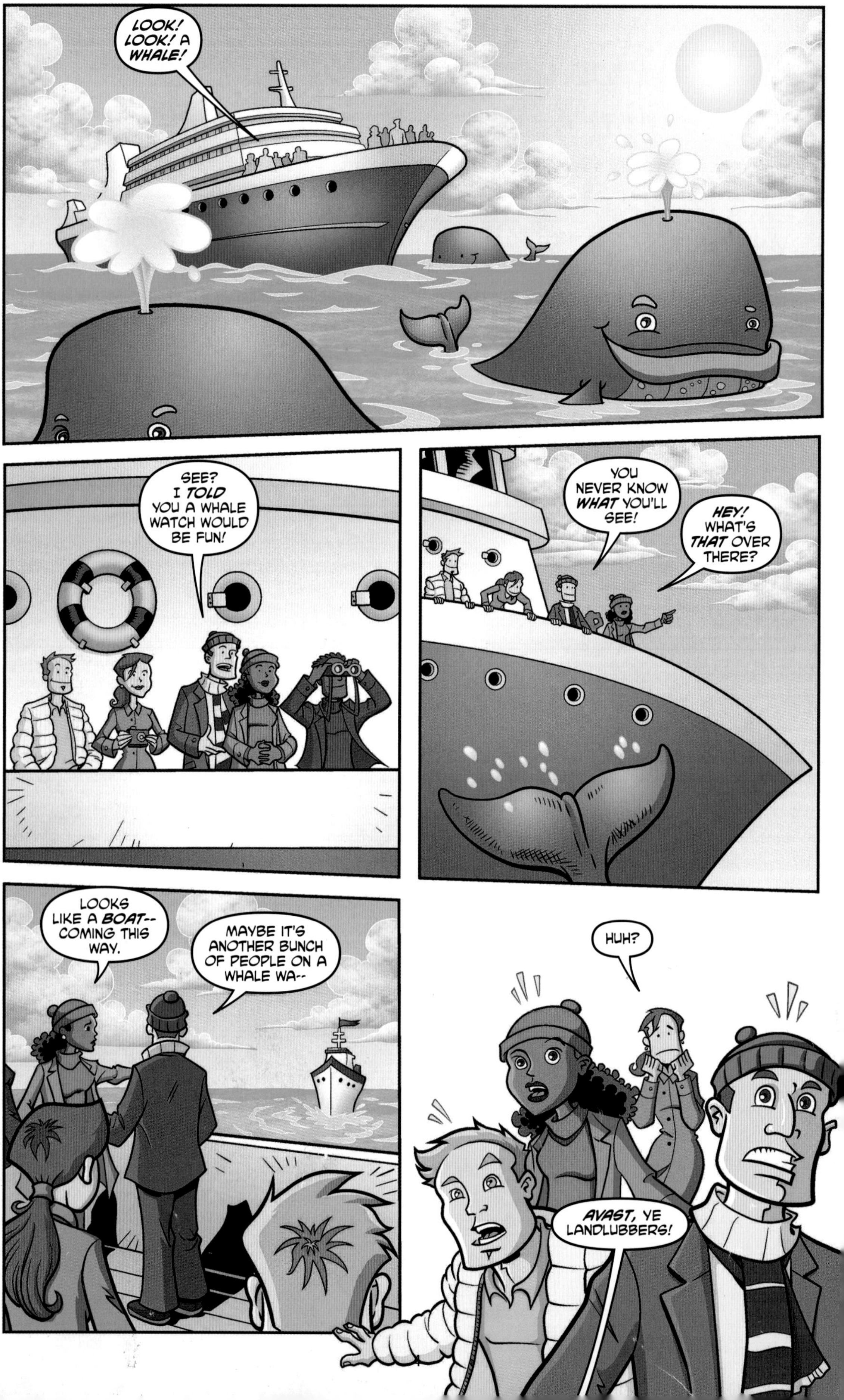
LOOK! LOOK! A WHALE!
SEE? I TOLD YOU A WHALE WATCH WOULD BE FUN!
YOU NEVER KNOW WHAT YOU'LL SEE!
HEY! WHAT'S THAT OVER THERE?
LOOKS LIKE A BOAT-- COMING THIS WAY.
MAYBE IT'S ANOTHER BUNCH OF PEOPLE ON A WHALE WA--
HUH?
AVAST, YE LANDLUBBERS!

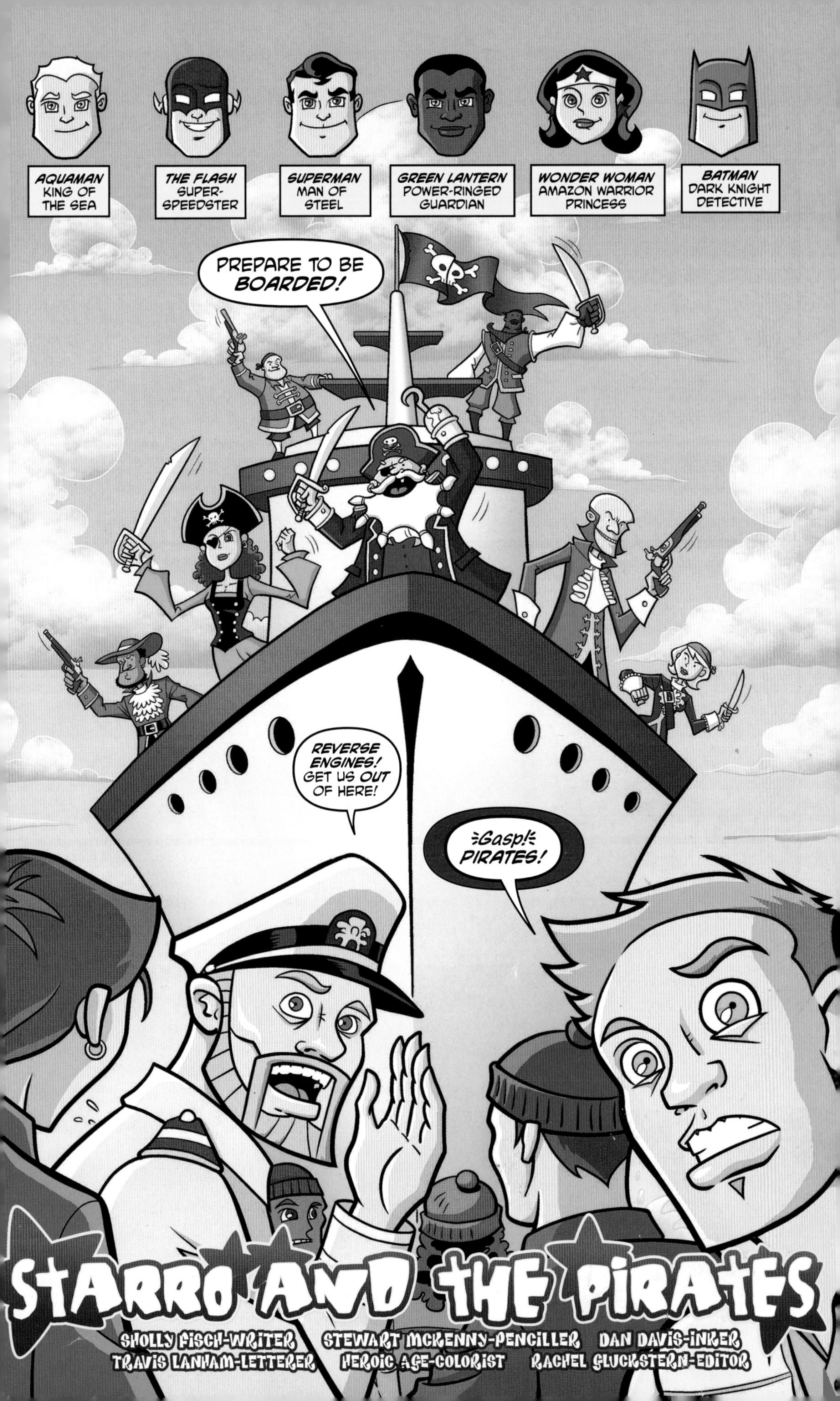

AQUAMAN
KING OF THE SEA
THE FLASH
SUPER-SPEEDSTER
SUPERMAN
MAN OF STEEL
GREEN LANTERN
POWER-RINGED GUARDIAN
WONDER WOMAN
AMAZON WARRIOR PRINCESS
BATMAN
DARK KNIGHT DETECTIVE
PREPARE TO BE BOARDED!
REVERSE ENGINES! GET US OUT OF HERE!
Gasp! PIRATES!
STARRO AND THE PIRATES
SHOLLY FISCH-WRITER
STEWART MCKENNY-PENCILLER
DAN DAVIS-INKER
TRAVIS LANHAM-LETTERER
HEROIC AGE-COLORIST
RACHEL GLUCKSTERN-EDITOR

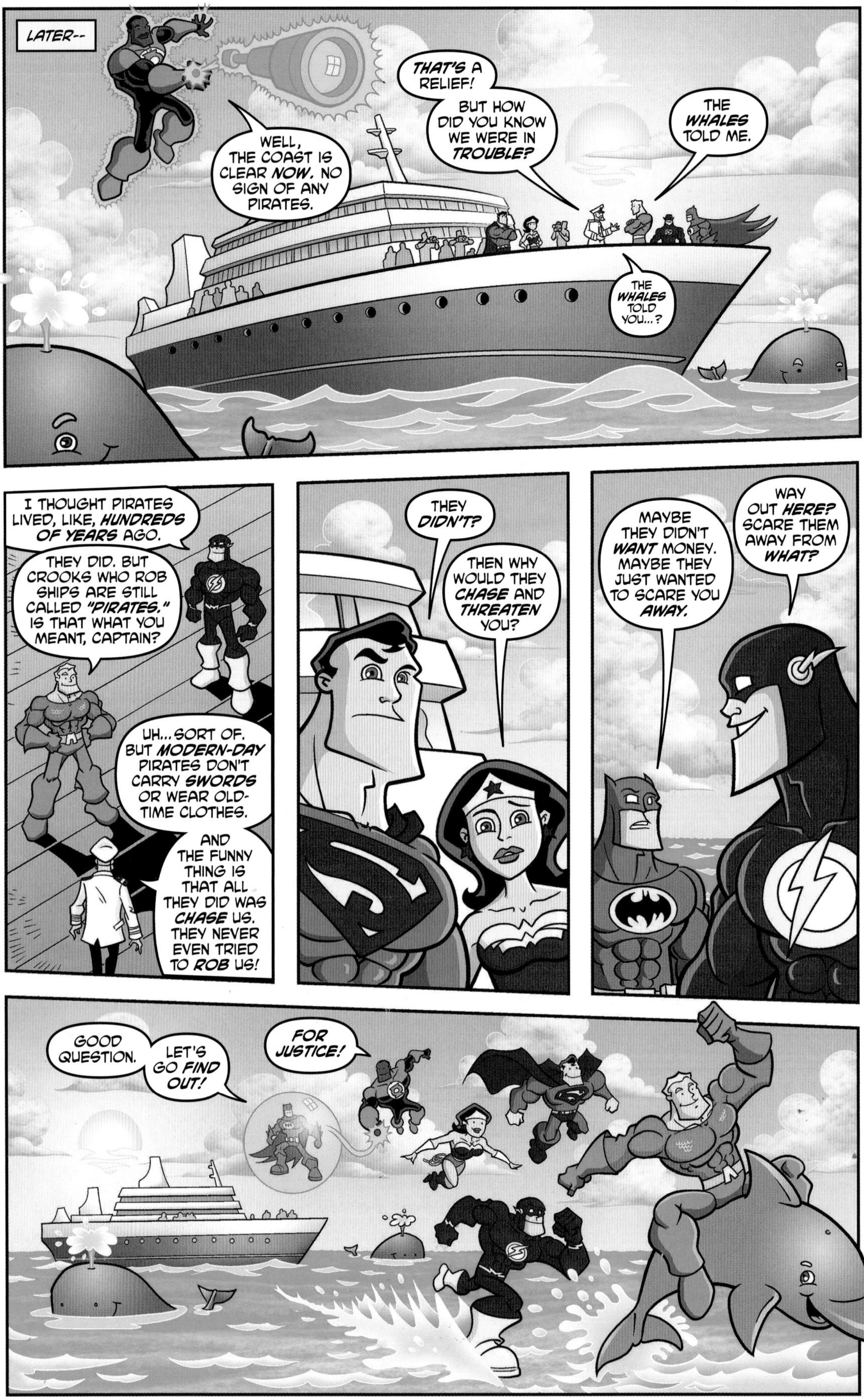
LATER--
WELL, THE COAST IS CLEAR NOW. NO SIGN OF ANY PIRATES.
THAT'S A RELIEF!
BUT HOW DID YOU KNOW WE WERE IN TROUBLE?
THE WHALES TOLD ME.
THE WHALES TOLD YOU...?
I THOUGHT PIRATES LIVED, LIKE, HUNDREDS OF YEARS AGO.
THEY DID. BUT CROOKS WHO ROB SHIPS ARE STILL CALLED "PIRATES." IS THAT WHAT YOU MEANT, CAPTAIN?
UH... SORT OF. BUT MODERN-DAY PIRATES DON'T CARRY SWORDS OR WEAR OLD-TIME CLOTHES.
AND THE FUNNY THING IS THAT ALL THEY DID WAS CHASE US. THEY NEVER EVEN TRIED TO ROB US!
THEY DIDN'T?
THEN WHY WOULD THEY CHASE AND THREATEN YOU?
MAYBE THEY DIDN'T WANT MONEY. MAYBE THEY JUST WANTED TO SCARE YOU AWAY.
WAY OUT HERE? SCARE THEM AWAY FROM WHAT?
GOOD QUESTION.
LET'S GO FIND OUT!
FOR JUSTICE!

LOOK! THERE'S SOMETHING *UP* AHEAD!

THEY'RE *RESEARCH PLATFORMS.* I HELPED *BUILD* THEM FOR SOME SCIENTISTS WHO ARE TRYING TO *PROTECT THE ENVIRONMENT.*

REALLY? ALL THAT *SMOKE* ISN'T HELPING THE ENVIRONMENT...

THE SMOKE SHOULDN'T *BE* THERE. THE SCIENTISTS BUILT THE PLATFORMS TO STUDY *GLACIERS* AND THE POLAR *ICE CAP.*

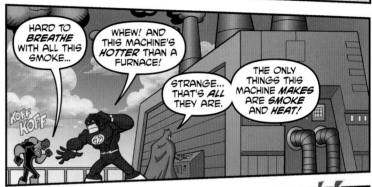

HARD TO *BREATHE* WITH ALL THIS SMOKE...

KOFF KOFF

WHEW! AND THIS MACHINE'S *HOTTER* THAN A FURNACE!

STRANGE... THAT'S *ALL* THEY ARE.

THE ONLY THINGS THIS MACHINE *MAKES* ARE *SMOKE* AND *HEAT!*

THIS CASE GETS *STRANGER* BY THE MOMENT! WHY WOULD SOMEONE BUILD MACHINES THAT DON'T *DO* ANYTHING?

AND WHY WOULD *PIRATES* KEEP SHIPS AWAY FROM THEM?

MAYBE WE SHOULD ASK *THEM!*

AVAST, YE SCURVY BILGE RATS! WE'LL *KEELHAUL* THE LOT OF YE!

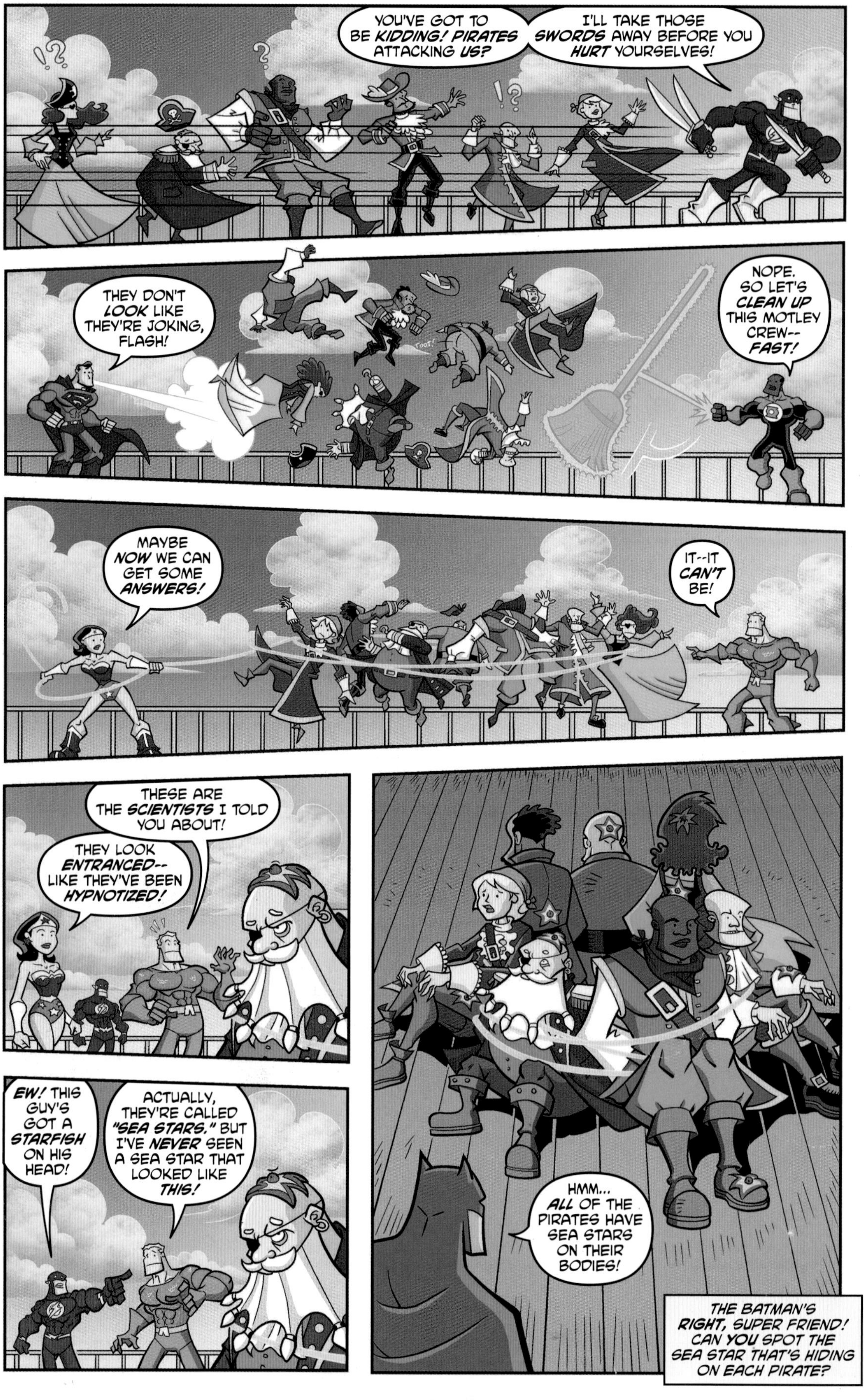
YOU'VE GOT TO BE KIDDING! PIRATES ATTACKING US?
I'LL TAKE THOSE SWORDS AWAY BEFORE YOU HURT YOURSELVES!
THEY DON'T LOOK LIKE THEY'RE JOKING, FLASH!
TOOT!
NOPE. SO LET'S CLEAN UP THIS MOTLEY CREW-- FAST!
MAYBE NOW WE CAN GET SOME ANSWERS!
IT--IT CAN'T BE!
THESE ARE THE SCIENTISTS I TOLD YOU ABOUT!
THEY LOOK ENTRANCED-- LIKE THEY'VE BEEN HYPNOTIZED!
EW! THIS GUY'S GOT A STARFISH ON HIS HEAD!
ACTUALLY, THEY'RE CALLED "SEA STARS," BUT I'VE NEVER SEEN A SEA STAR THAT LOOKED LIKE THIS!
HMM... ALL OF THE PIRATES HAVE SEA STARS ON THEIR BODIES!
THE BATMAN'S RIGHT, SUPER FRIEND! CAN YOU SPOT THE SEA STAR THAT'S HIDING ON EACH PIRATE?

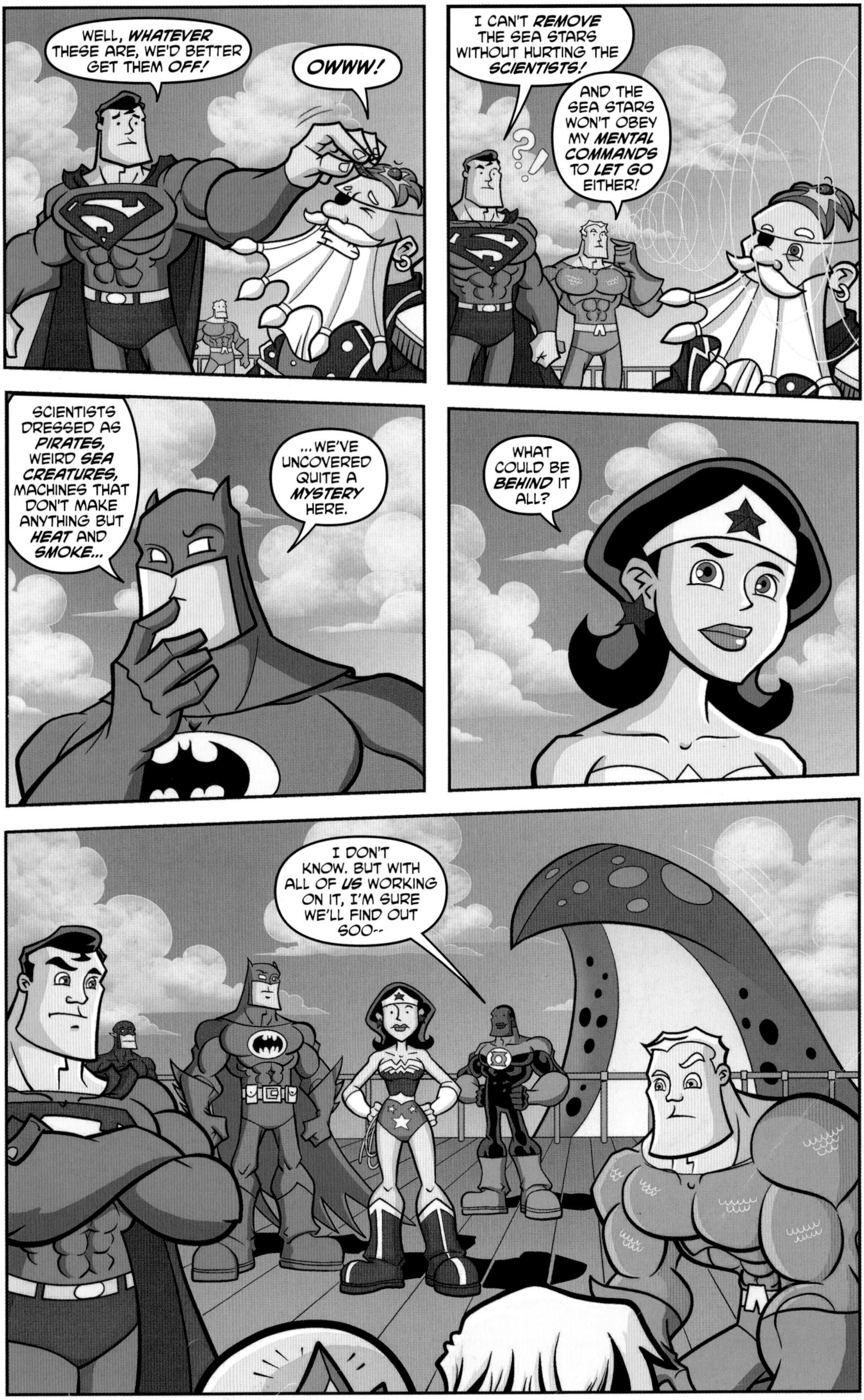

WELL, WHATEVER THESE ARE, WE'D BETTER GET THEM OFF!
OWWW!
I CAN'T REMOVE THE SEA STARS WITHOUT HURTING THE SCIENTISTS!
AND THE SEA STARS WON'T OBEY MY MENTAL COMMANDS TO LET GO EITHER!
SCIENTISTS DRESSED AS PIRATES, WEIRD SEA CREATURES, MACHINES THAT DON'T MAKE ANYTHING BUT HEAT AND SMOKE...
...WE'VE UNCOVERED QUITE A MYSTERY HERE.
WHAT COULD BE BEHIND IT ALL?
I DON'T KNOW. BUT WITH ALL OF US WORKING ON IT, I'M SURE WE'LL FIND OUT SOO--

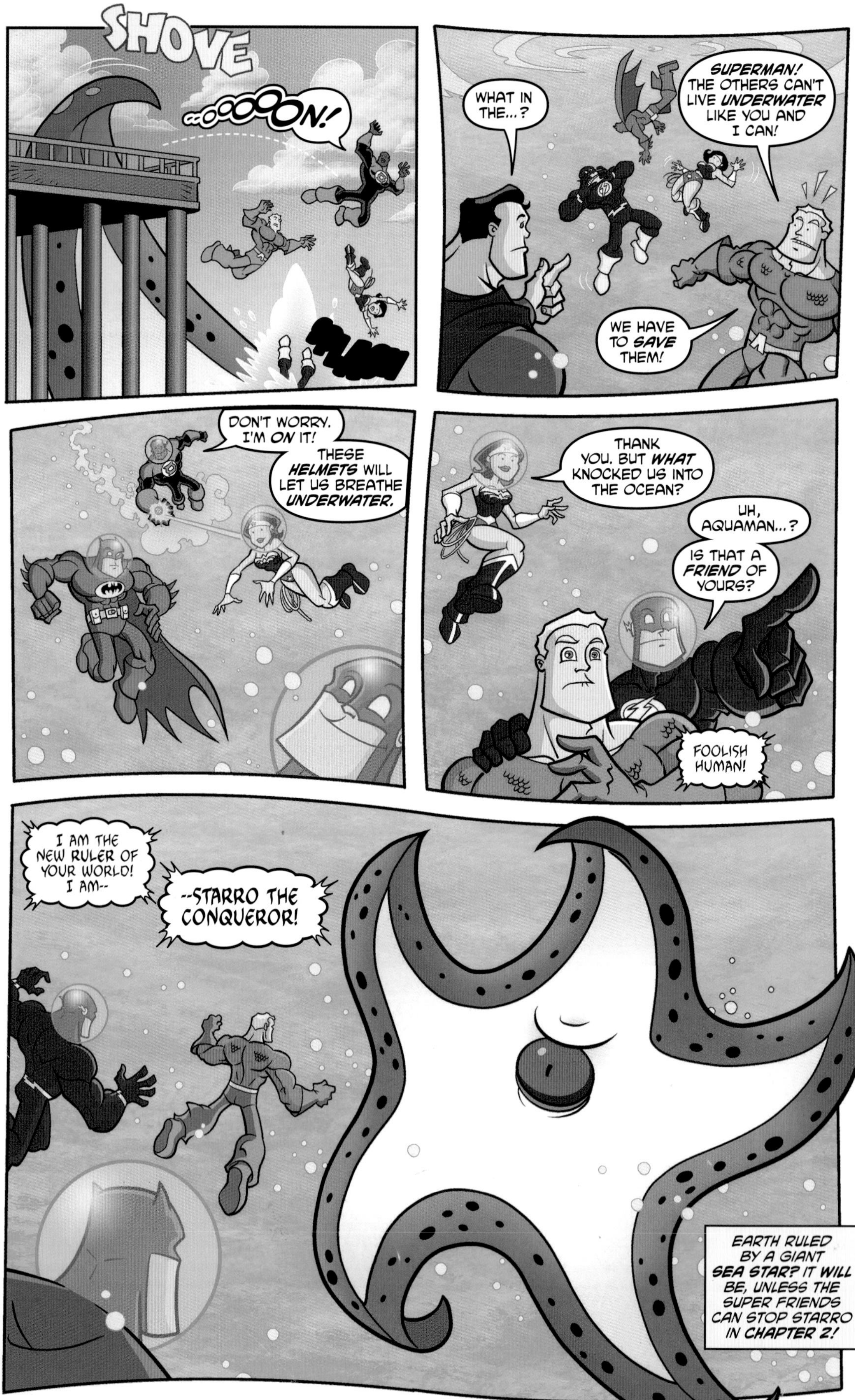
SHOVE
--OOOOON!
SPLUSH
WHAT IN THE...?
SUPERMAN! THE OTHERS CAN'T LIVE UNDERWATER LIKE YOU AND I CAN!
WE HAVE TO SAVE THEM!
DON'T WORRY. I'M ON IT!
THESE HELMETS WILL LET US BREATHE UNDERWATER.
THANK YOU. BUT WHAT KNOCKED US INTO THE OCEAN?
UH, AQUAMAN...?
IS THAT A FRIEND OF YOURS?
FOOLISH HUMAN!
I AM THE NEW RULER OF YOUR WORLD! I AM--
--STARRO THE CONQUEROR!
EARTH RULED BY A GIANT SEA STAR? IT WILL BE, UNLESS THE SUPER FRIENDS CAN STOP STARRO IN CHAPTER 2!

STARRO AND THE PIRATES CHAPTER 2

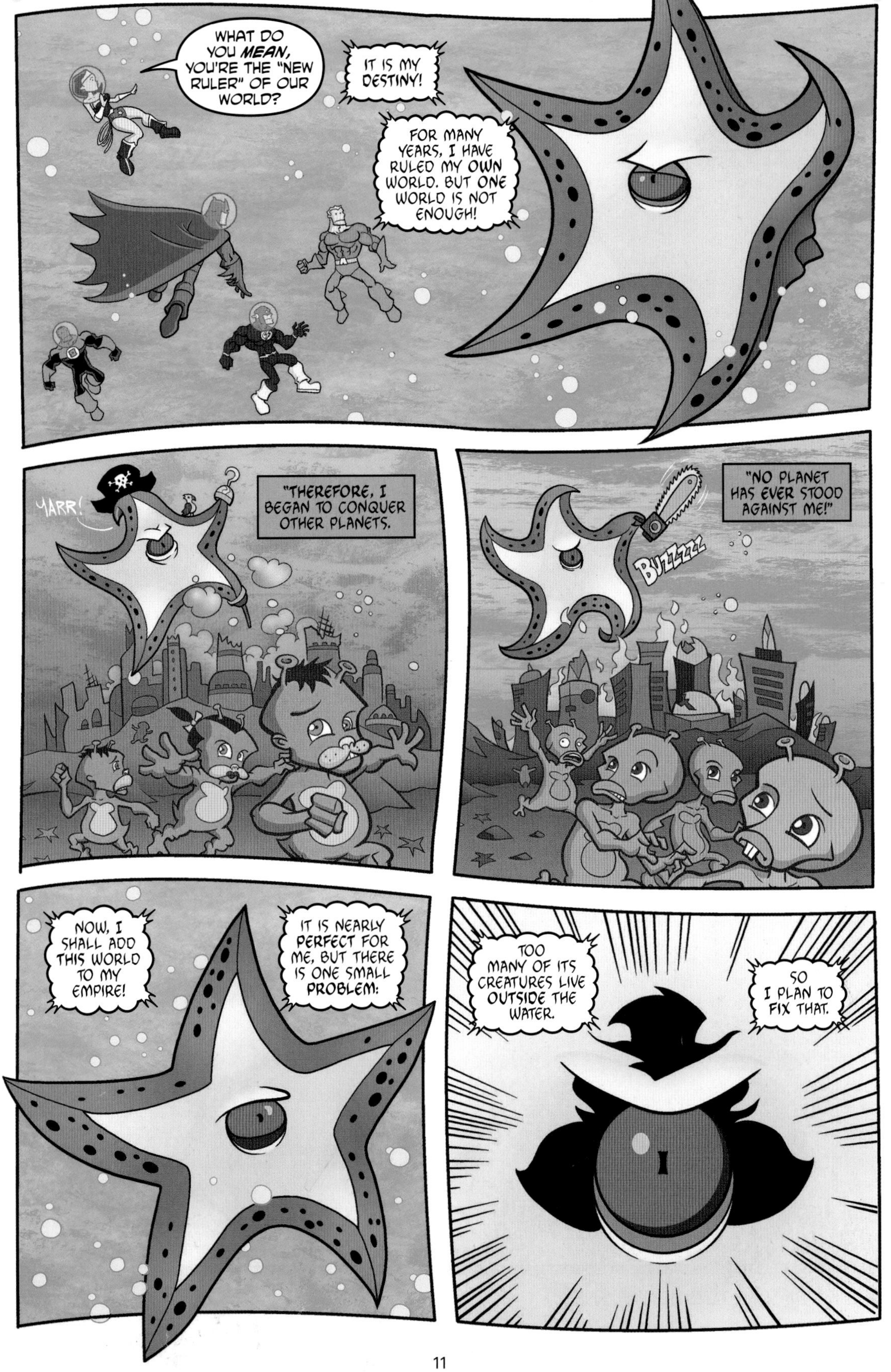
WHAT DO YOU *MEAN*, YOU'RE THE "NEW RULER" OF OUR WORLD?
IT IS MY DESTINY!
FOR MANY YEARS, I HAVE RULED MY OWN WORLD. BUT ONE WORLD IS NOT ENOUGH!
YARR!
"THEREFORE, I BEGAN TO CONQUER OTHER PLANETS.
"NO PLANET HAS EVER STOOD AGAINST ME!"
BUZZZZZ
NOW, I SHALL ADD THIS WORLD TO MY EMPIRE!
IT IS NEARLY PERFECT FOR ME, BUT THERE IS ONE SMALL PROBLEM:
TOO MANY OF ITS CREATURES LIVE OUTSIDE THE WATER.
SO I PLAN TO FIX THAT.

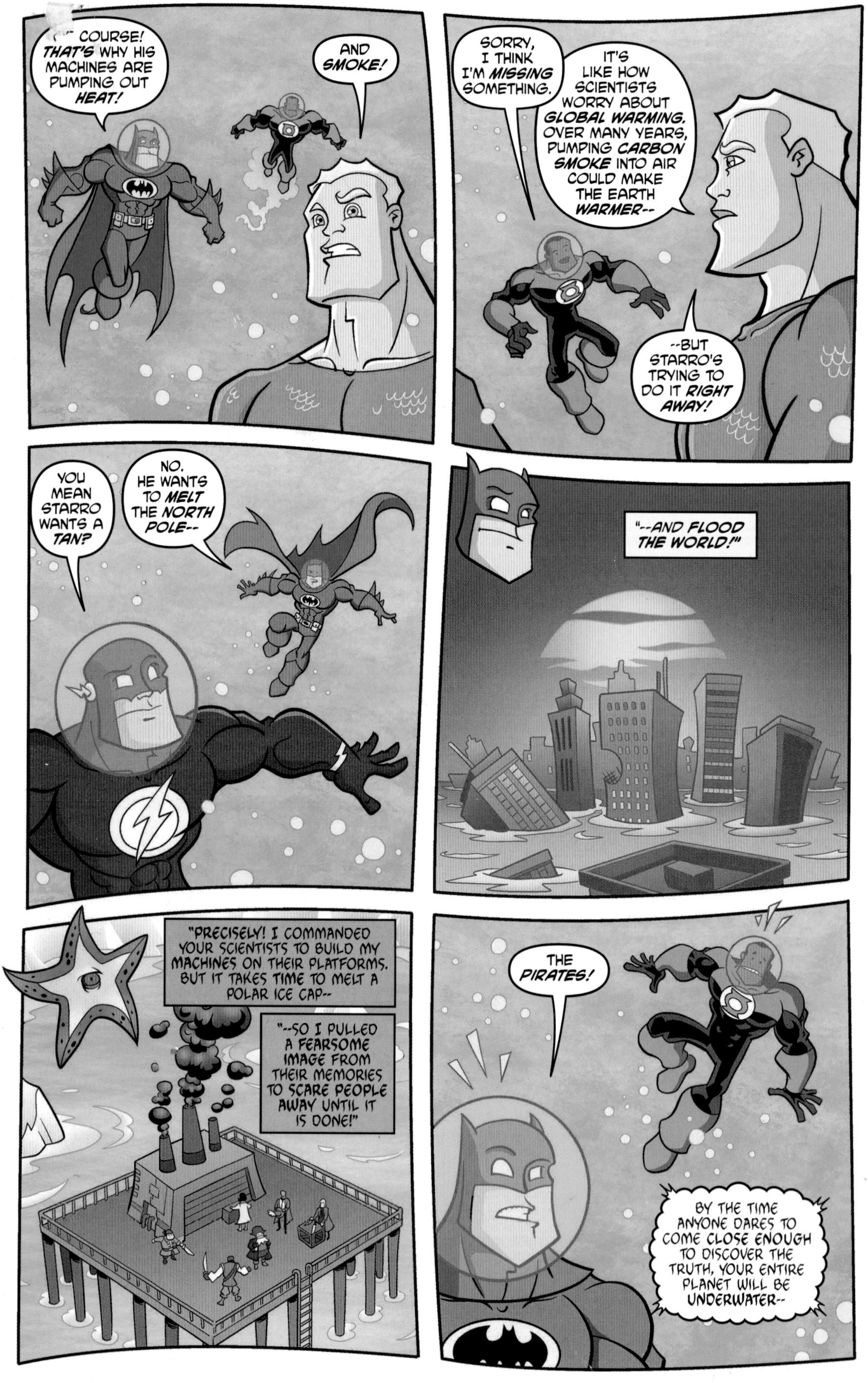

OF COURSE! THAT'S WHY HIS MACHINES ARE PUMPING OUT HEAT!
AND SMOKE!
SORRY, I THINK I'M MISSING SOMETHING.
IT'S LIKE HOW SCIENTISTS WORRY ABOUT GLOBAL WARMING. OVER MANY YEARS, PUMPING CARBON SMOKE INTO AIR COULD MAKE THE EARTH WARMER--
--BUT STARRO'S TRYING TO DO IT RIGHT AWAY!
YOU MEAN STARRO WANTS A TAN?
NO. HE WANTS TO MELT THE NORTH POLE--
"--AND FLOOD THE WORLD!"
"PRECISELY! I COMMANDED YOUR SCIENTISTS TO BUILD MY MACHINES ON THEIR PLATFORMS. BUT IT TAKES TIME TO MELT A POLAR ICE CAP--
"--SO I PULLED A FEARSOME IMAGE FROM THEIR MEMORIES TO SCARE PEOPLE AWAY UNTIL IT IS DONE!"
THE PIRATES!
BY THE TIME ANYONE DARES TO COME CLOSE ENOUGH TO DISCOVER THE TRUTH, YOUR ENTIRE PLANET WILL BE UNDERWATER--

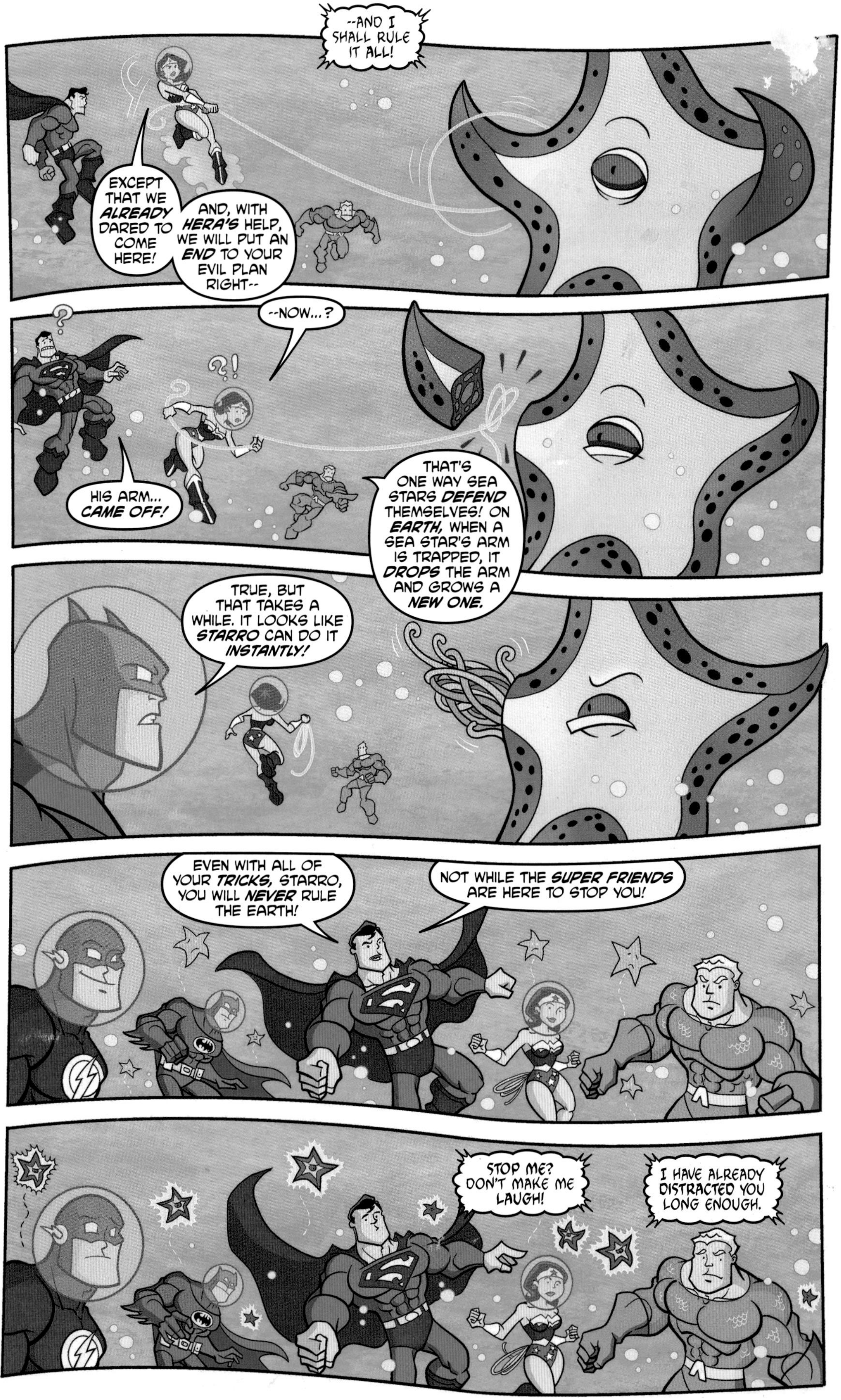
--AND I SHALL RULE IT ALL!
EXCEPT THAT WE ALREADY DARED TO COME HERE!
AND, WITH HERA'S HELP, WE WILL PUT AN END TO YOUR EVIL PLAN RIGHT--
--NOW...?
?!
HIS ARM... CAME OFF!
THAT'S ONE WAY SEA STARS DEFEND THEMSELVES! ON EARTH, WHEN A SEA STAR'S ARM IS TRAPPED, IT DROPS THE ARM AND GROWS A NEW ONE.
TRUE, BUT THAT TAKES A WHILE. IT LOOKS LIKE STARRO CAN DO IT INSTANTLY!
EVEN WITH ALL OF YOUR TRICKS, STARRO, YOU WILL NEVER RULE THE EARTH!
NOT WHILE THE SUPER FRIENDS ARE HERE TO STOP YOU!
STOP ME? DON'T MAKE ME LAUGH!
I HAVE ALREADY DISTRACTED YOU LONG ENOUGH.

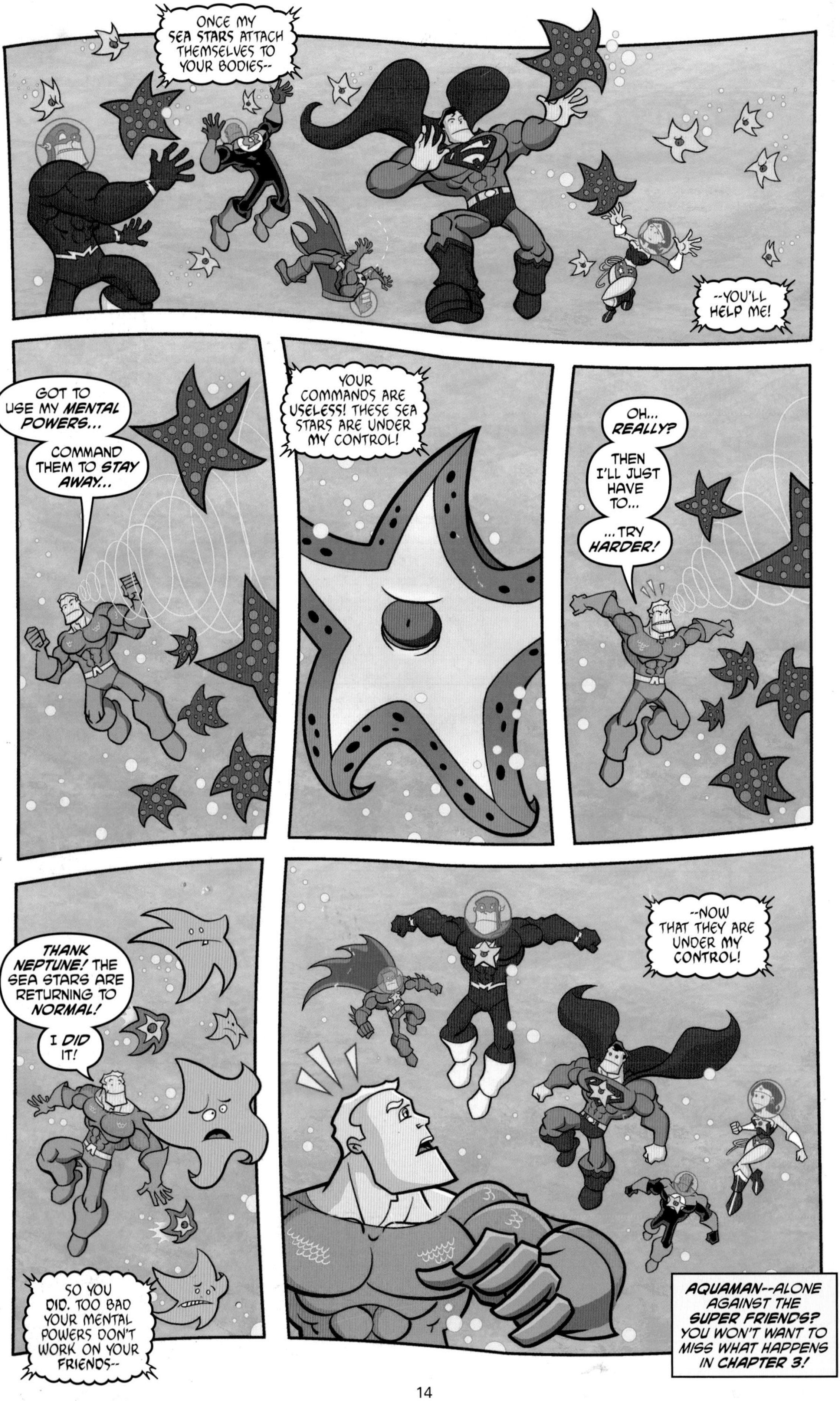

ONCE MY SEA STARS ATTACH THEMSELVES TO YOUR BODIES--
--YOU'LL HELP ME!
GOT TO USE MY *MENTAL POWERS...*
COMMAND THEM TO *STAY AWAY...*
YOUR COMMANDS ARE USELESS! THESE SEA STARS ARE UNDER MY CONTROL!
OH... *REALLY?*
THEN I'LL JUST HAVE TO...
...TRY *HARDER!*
THANK NEPTUNE! THE SEA STARS ARE RETURNING TO *NORMAL!*
I *DID* IT!
SO YOU DID. TOO BAD YOUR MENTAL POWERS DON'T WORK ON YOUR FRIENDS--
--NOW THAT THEY ARE UNDER MY CONTROL!
AQUAMAN--ALONE AGAINST THE SUPER FRIENDS? YOU WON'T WANT TO MISS WHAT HAPPENS IN CHAPTER 3!

STARRO AND THE PIRATES CHAPTER 3

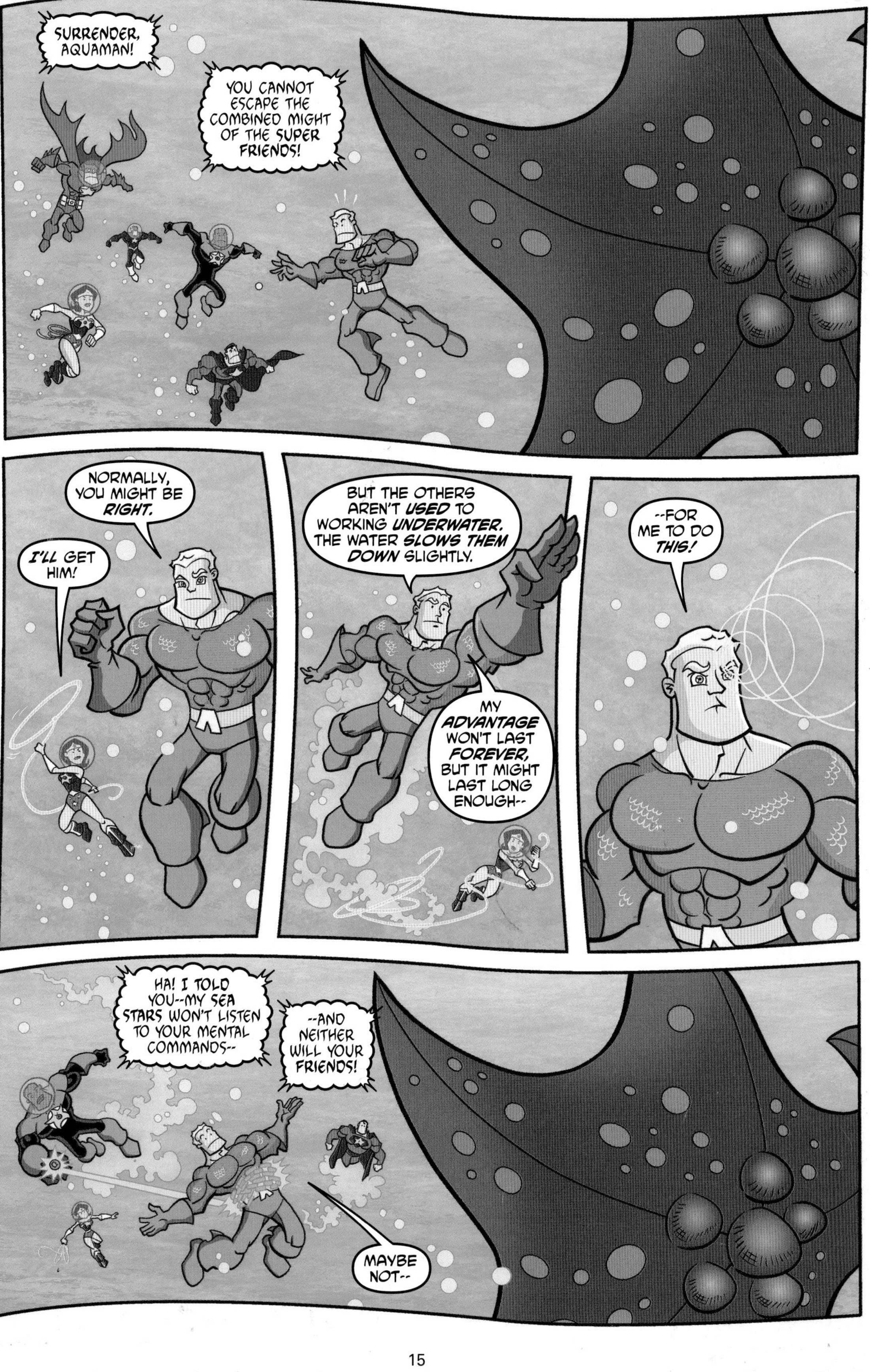
SURRENDER, AQUAMAN!
YOU CANNOT ESCAPE THE COMBINED MIGHT OF THE SUPER FRIENDS!
NORMALLY, YOU MIGHT BE *RIGHT.*
I'LL GET HIM!
BUT THE OTHERS AREN'T *USED* TO WORKING *UNDERWATER.* THE WATER *SLOWS THEM DOWN* SLIGHTLY.
MY *ADVANTAGE* WON'T LAST *FOREVER,* BUT IT MIGHT LAST LONG ENOUGH--
--FOR ME TO DO *THIS!*
HA! I TOLD YOU--MY SEA STARS WON'T LISTEN TO YOUR MENTAL COMMANDS--
--AND NEITHER WILL YOUR FRIENDS!
MAYBE NOT--

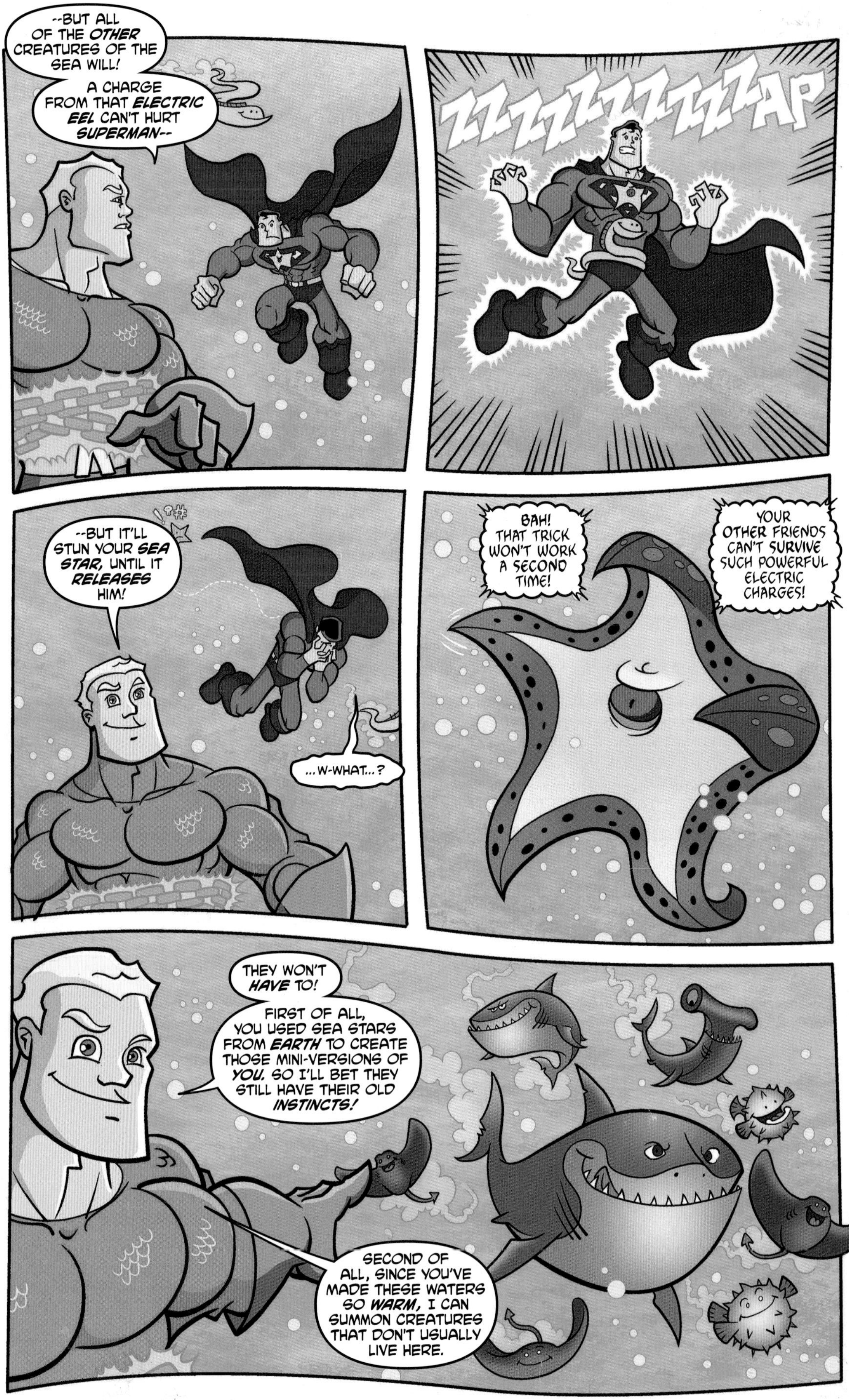
--BUT ALL OF THE OTHER CREATURES OF THE SEA WILL!
A CHARGE FROM THAT ELECTRIC EEL CAN'T HURT SUPERMAN--
ZZZZZZZZZZZAP
--BUT IT'LL STUN YOUR SEA STAR, UNTIL IT RELEASES HIM!
...W-WHAT...?
BAH! THAT TRICK WON'T WORK A SECOND TIME!
YOUR OTHER FRIENDS CAN'T SURVIVE SUCH POWERFUL ELECTRIC CHARGES!
THEY WON'T HAVE TO!
FIRST OF ALL, YOU USED SEA STARS FROM EARTH TO CREATE THOSE MINI-VERSIONS OF YOU. SO I'LL BET THEY STILL HAVE THEIR OLD INSTINCTS!
SECOND OF ALL, SINCE YOU'VE MADE THESE WATERS SO WARM, I CAN SUMMON CREATURES THAT DON'T USUALLY LIVE HERE.

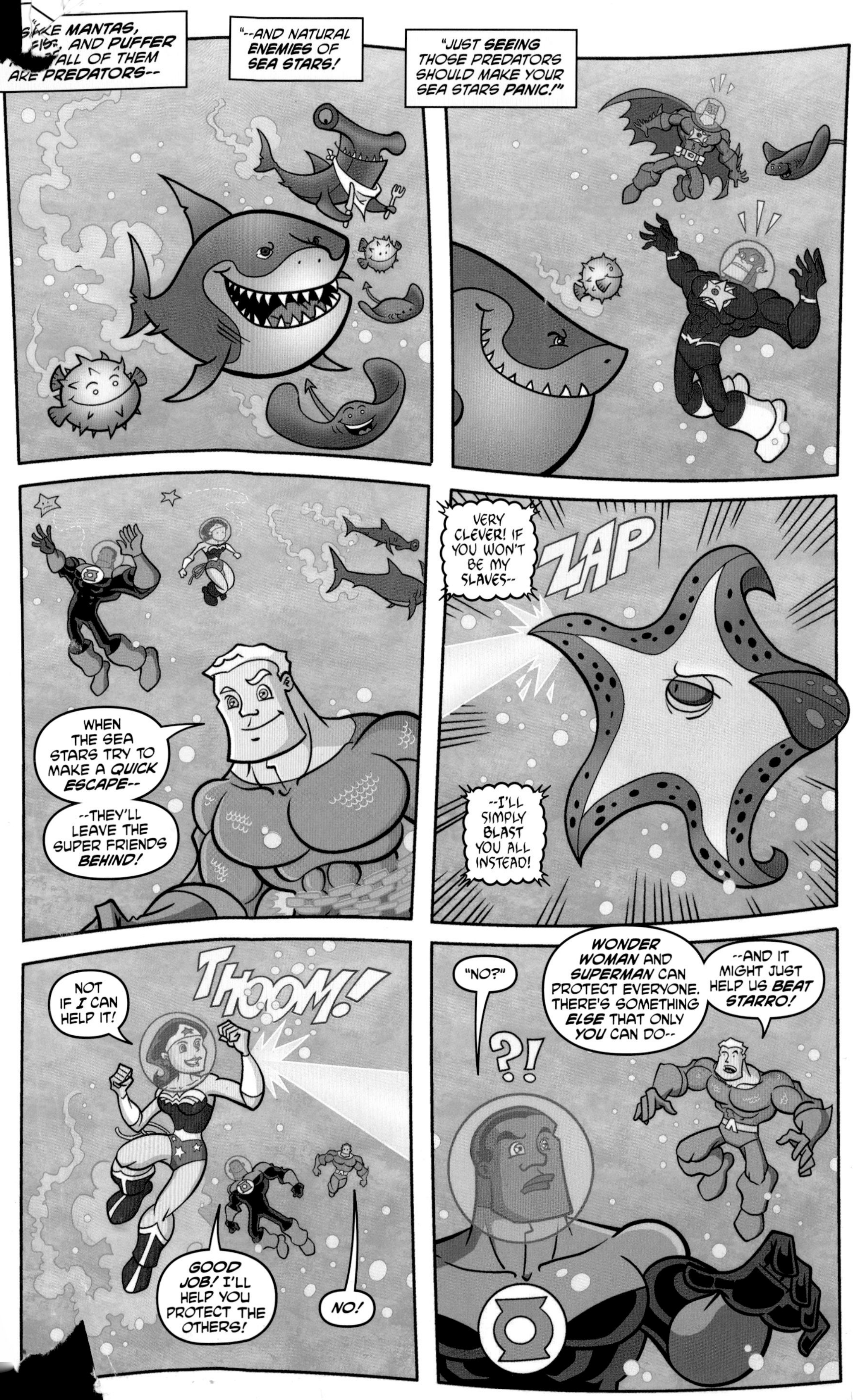
MANTAS,
AND PUFFER
ALL OF THEM
ARE PREDATORS--
"--AND NATURAL ENEMIES OF SEA STARS!
"JUST SEEING THOSE PREDATORS SHOULD MAKE YOUR SEA STARS PANIC!"
WHEN THE SEA STARS TRY TO MAKE A QUICK ESCAPE--
--THEY'LL LEAVE THE SUPER FRIENDS BEHIND!
VERY CLEVER! IF YOU WON'T BE MY SLAVES--
ZAP
--I'LL SIMPLY BLAST YOU ALL INSTEAD!
NOT IF I CAN HELP IT!
THOOM!
GOOD JOB! I'LL HELP YOU PROTECT THE OTHERS!
NO!
"NO?"
?!
WONDER WOMAN AND SUPERMAN CAN PROTECT EVERYONE. THERE'S SOMETHING ELSE THAT ONLY YOU CAN DO--
--AND IT MIGHT JUST HELP US BEAT STARRO!

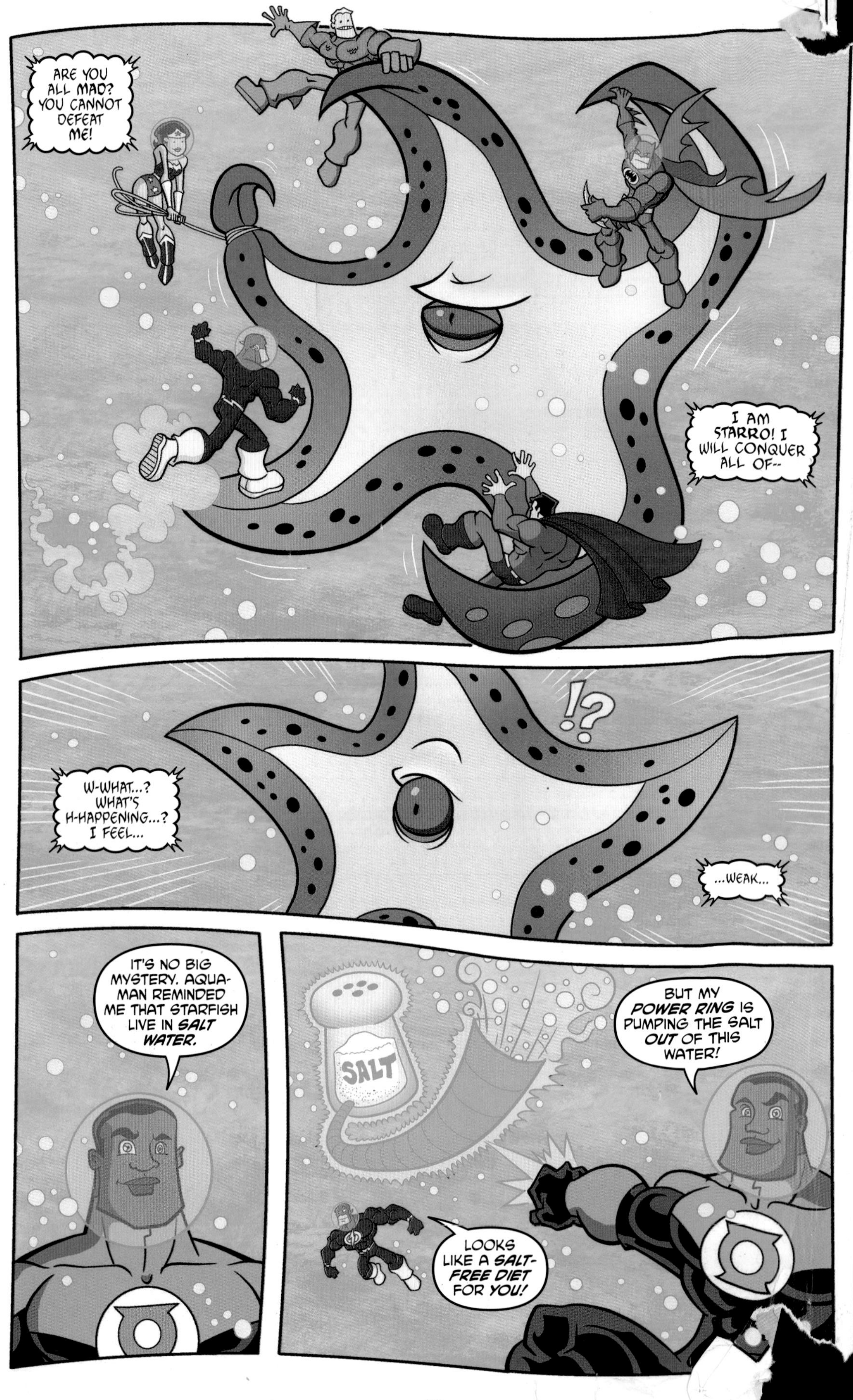
ARE YOU ALL MAD? YOU CANNOT DEFEAT ME!
I AM STARRO! I WILL CONQUER ALL OF--
!?
W-WHAT...? WHAT'S H-HAPPENING...? I FEEL...
...WEAK...
IT'S NO BIG MYSTERY. AQUA-MAN REMINDED ME THAT STARFISH LIVE IN *SALT WATER.*
SALT
BUT MY *POWER RING* IS PUMPING THE SALT *OUT* OF THIS WATER!
LOOKS LIKE A *SALT-FREE DIET* FOR *YOU!*

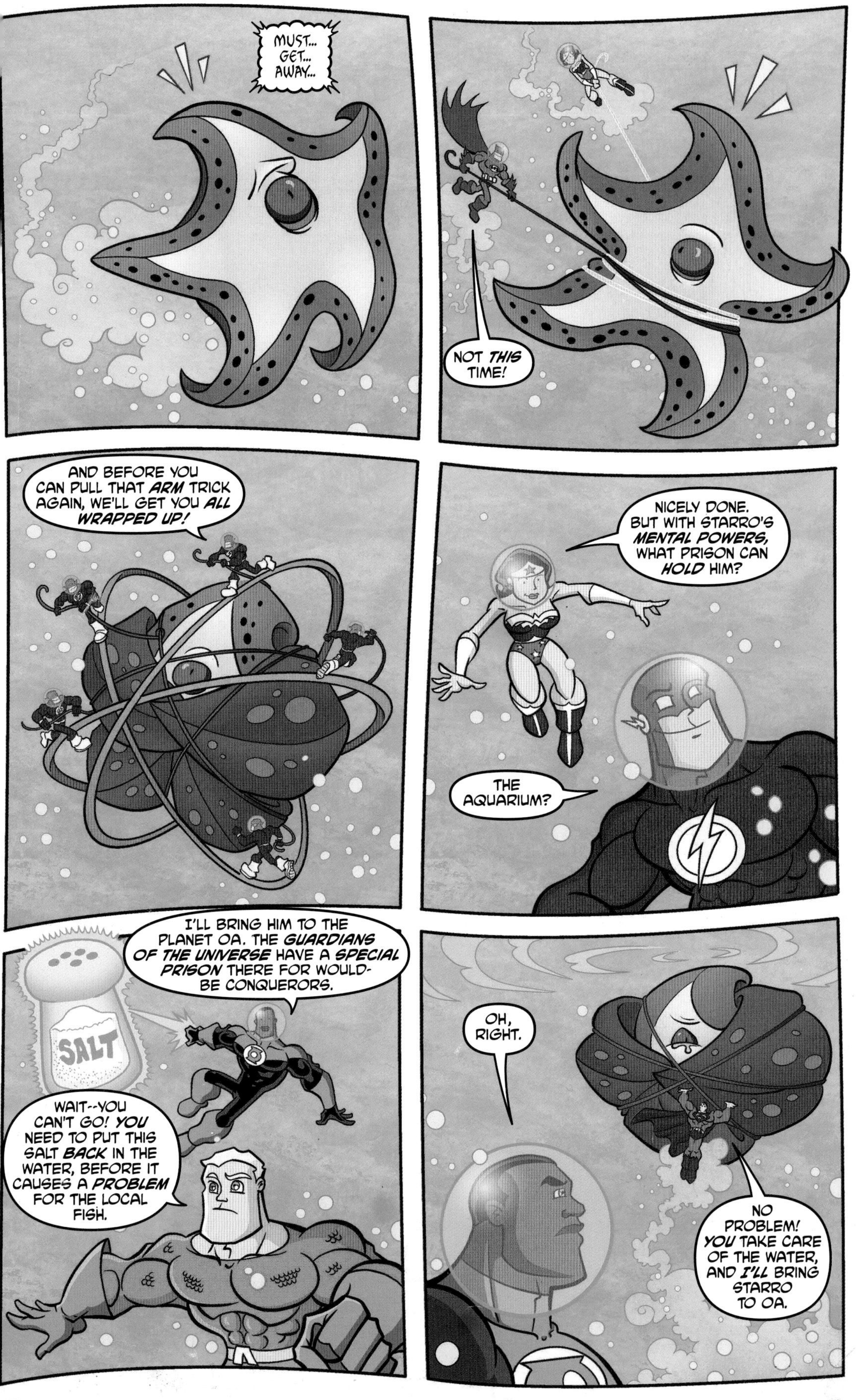
MUST... GET... AWAY...
NOT THIS TIME!
AND BEFORE YOU CAN PULL THAT ARM TRICK AGAIN, WE'LL GET YOU ALL WRAPPED UP!
NICELY DONE. BUT WITH STARRO'S MENTAL POWERS, WHAT PRISON CAN HOLD HIM?
THE AQUARIUM?
I'LL BRING HIM TO THE PLANET OA. THE GUARDIANS OF THE UNIVERSE HAVE A SPECIAL PRISON THERE FOR WOULD-BE CONQUERORS.
SALT
WAIT--YOU CAN'T GO! YOU NEED TO PUT THIS SALT BACK IN THE WATER, BEFORE IT CAUSES A PROBLEM FOR THE LOCAL FISH.
OH, RIGHT.
NO PROBLEM! YOU TAKE CARE OF THE WATER, AND I'LL BRING STARRO TO OA.

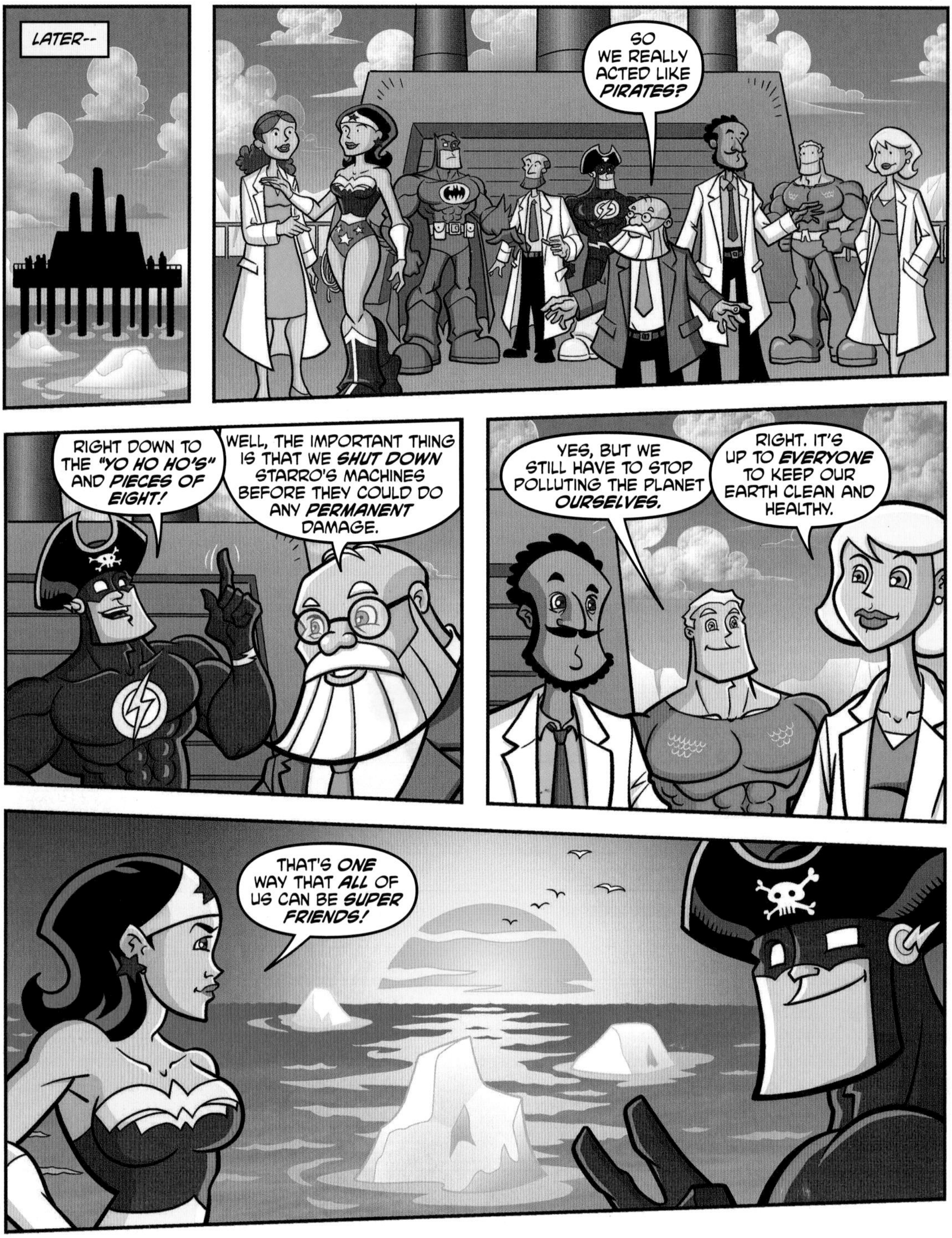
LATER--
SO WE REALLY ACTED LIKE PIRATES?
RIGHT DOWN TO THE "YO HO HO'S" AND PIECES OF EIGHT!
WELL, THE IMPORTANT THING IS THAT WE SHUT DOWN STARRO'S MACHINES BEFORE THEY COULD DO ANY PERMANENT DAMAGE.
YES, BUT WE STILL HAVE TO STOP POLLUTING THE PLANET OURSELVES.
RIGHT. IT'S UP TO EVERYONE TO KEEP OUR EARTH CLEAN AND HEALTHY.
THAT'S ONE WAY THAT ALL OF US CAN BE SUPER FRIENDS!

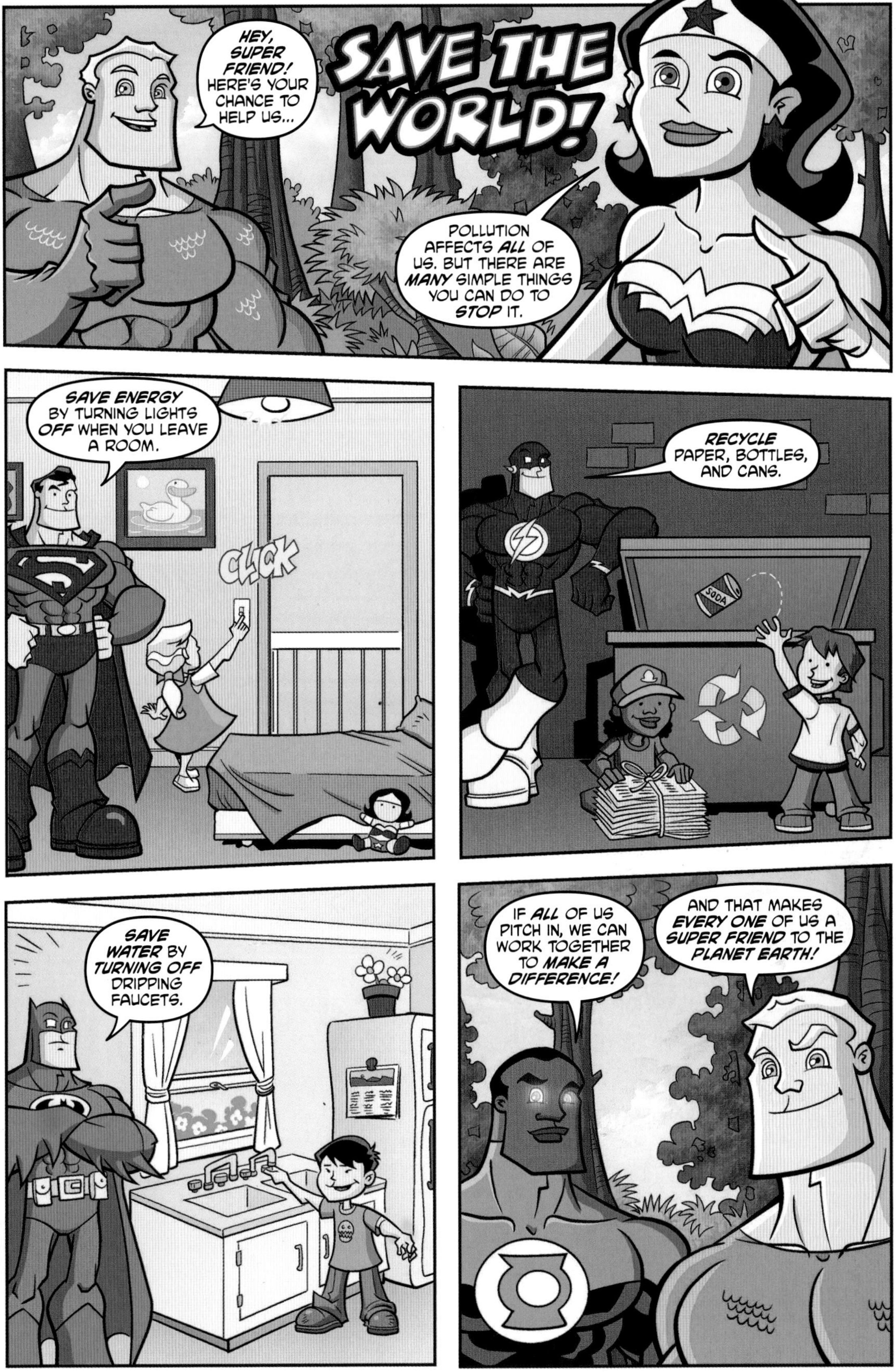
HEY, SUPER FRIEND! HERE'S YOUR CHANCE TO HELP US...
SAVE THE WORLD!
POLLUTION AFFECTS ALL OF US. BUT THERE ARE MANY SIMPLE THINGS YOU CAN DO TO STOP IT.
SAVE ENERGY BY TURNING LIGHTS OFF WHEN YOU LEAVE A ROOM.
CLICK
RECYCLE PAPER, BOTTLES, AND CANS.
SODA
SAVE WATER BY TURNING OFF DRIPPING FAUCETS.
IF ALL OF US PITCH IN, WE CAN WORK TOGETHER TO MAKE A DIFFERENCE!
AND THAT MAKES EVERY ONE OF US A SUPER FRIEND TO THE PLANET EARTH!

ATTENTION, ALL SUPER FRIENDS!

HERE'S THIS BOOK'S SECRET MESSAGE:

PEVOY CYSOXRP ZBBU BEI CBY BINOYP

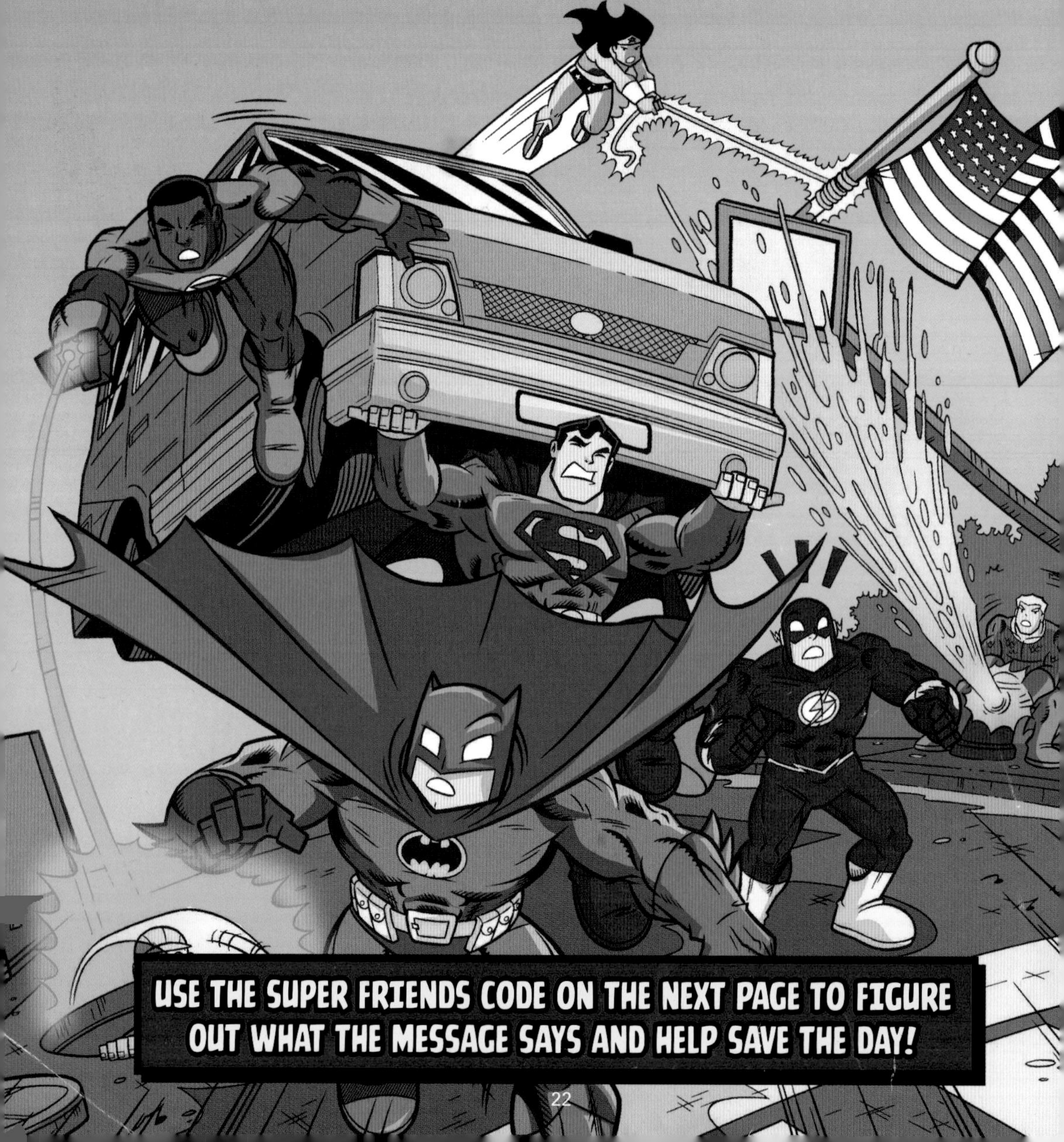

USE THE SUPER FRIENDS CODE ON THE NEXT PAGE TO FIGURE OUT WHAT THE MESSAGE SAYS AND HELP SAVE THE DAY!

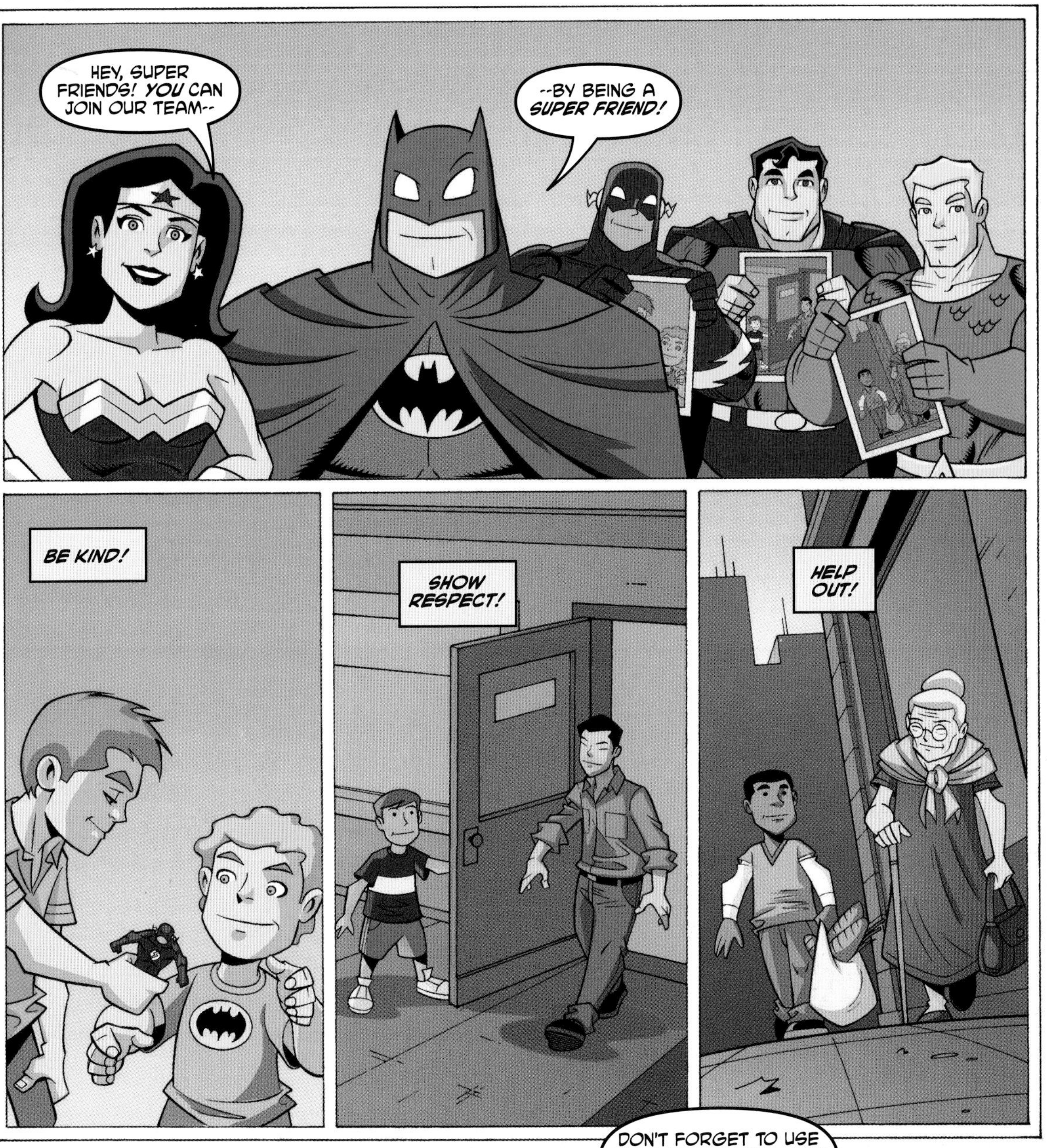
HEY, SUPER FRIENDS! YOU CAN JOIN OUR TEAM--
--BY BEING A SUPER FRIEND!
BE KIND!
SHOW RESPECT!
HELP OUT!

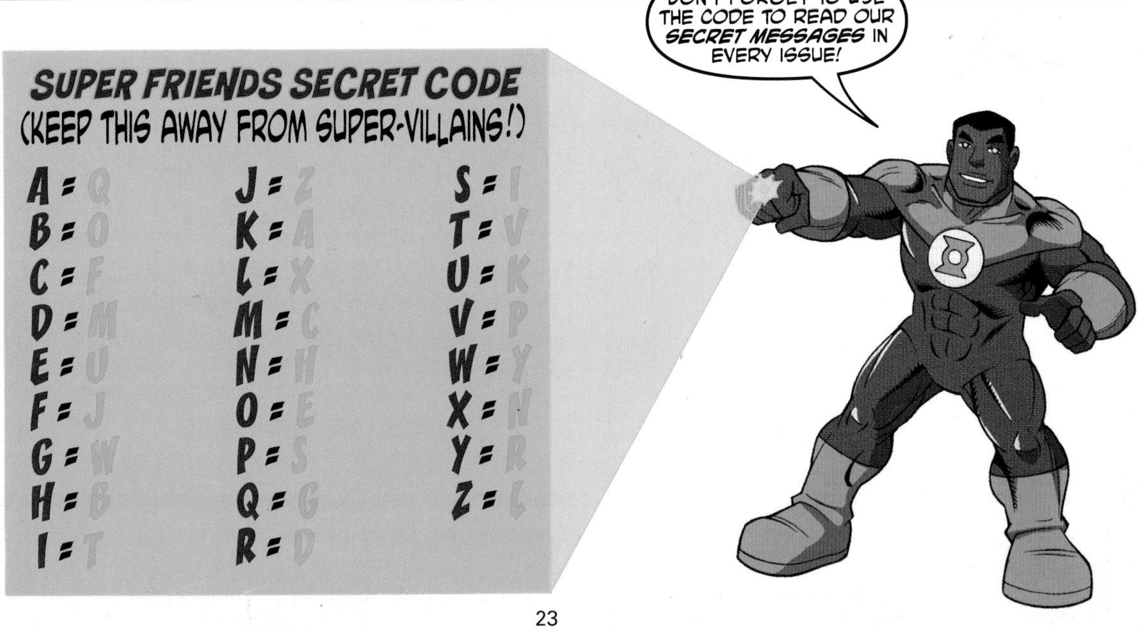
DON'T FORGET TO USE THE CODE TO READ OUR SECRET MESSAGES IN EVERY ISSUE!
SUPER FRIENDS SECRET CODE
(KEEP THIS AWAY FROM SUPER-VILLAINS!)
A = Q
B = O
C = F
D = M
E = U
F = J
G = W
H = B
I = T
J = Z
K = A
L = X
M = C
N = H
O = E
P = S
Q = G
R = D
S = I
T = V
U = K
V = P
W = Y
X = N
Y = R
Z = L

KNOW YOUR SUPER FRIENDS!

SUPERMAN

Real Name: Clark Kent

Powers: Super-strength, super-speed, flight, super-senses, heat vision, invulnerability, super-breath

Origin: Just before the planet Krypton exploded, baby Kal-EL escaped in a rocket to Earth. On Earth, he was adopted by a kind couple named Jonathan and Martha Kent.

BATMAN

Secret Identity: Bruce Wayne

Abilities: World's greatest detective, acrobat, escape artist

Origin: Orphaned at a young age, young millionaire Bruce Wayne promised to keep all people safe from crime. After training for many years, he put on costume that would scare criminals – the costume of Batman.

WONDER WOMAN

Secret Identity: Princess Diana

Powers: Super-strong, faster than normal humans, uses her bracelets as shields and magic lasso to make people tell the truth

Origin: Diana is the Princess of Paradise Island, the hidden home of the Amazons. When Diana was a baby, the Greek gods gave her special powers.

GREEN LANTERN

Secret Identity: John Stewart

Powers: Through the strength of willpower, Green Lantern's power ring can create anything he imagines

Origin: Led by the Guardians of the Universe, the Green Lantern Corps is an outer-space police force that keeps the whole universe safe. The Guardians chose John to protect Earth as our planet's Green Lantern.

THE FLASH

Secret Identity: Wally West

Powers: Flash uses his super-speed in many ways: he can run across water or up the side of a building, spin around to make a tornado, or vibrate his body to walk right through a wall

Origin: As a boy, Wally West became the super-fast Kid Flash when lightning hit a rack of chemicals that spilled on him. Today, he helps others as the Flash.

AQUAMAN

Real Name: King Orin or Arthur Curry

Powers: Breathes underwater, communicates with fish, swims at high speed, stronger than normal humans

Origin: Orin's father was a lighthouse keeper and his mother was a mermaid from the undersea land of Atlantis. As Orin grew up, he learned that he could live on land and underwater. He decided to use his powers to keep the seven seas safe as Aquaman.

CREATORS

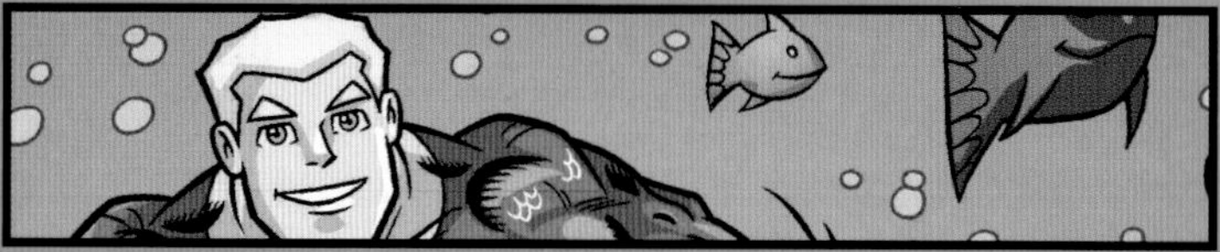

SHOLLY FISCH WRITER

Bitten by a radioactive typewriter, Sholly Fisch has spent the wee hours writing books, comics, TV scripts, and online material for more than 25 years. His comic book credits include more than 200 stories and features about characters such as Batman, Superman, Bugs Bunny, Daffy Duck, Spider-Man, and Ben 10. Currently, he writes stories for Action Comics every month, plus stories for Looney Tunes and Scooby-Doo. By day, Sholly is a mild-mannered developmental psychologist who helps to create educational TV shows, websites, and other media for kids.

STEWART MCKENNY ARTIST

Stewart McKenny has illustrated a variety of comic books and characters. He prides himself on his ability to adapt to new styles of illustration for Dark Horse, Marvel, and especially DC Comics.

DAN DAVIS ARTIST

Dan Davis has illustrated the Garfield comic series as well as books for Warner Bros. and DC Comics. He has brought a variety of comic book characters to life, including Batman and the rest of the Super Friends! In 2012, Dan was nominated for an Eisner award for the Batman Brave and the Bold series. He currently resides in Gotham City.

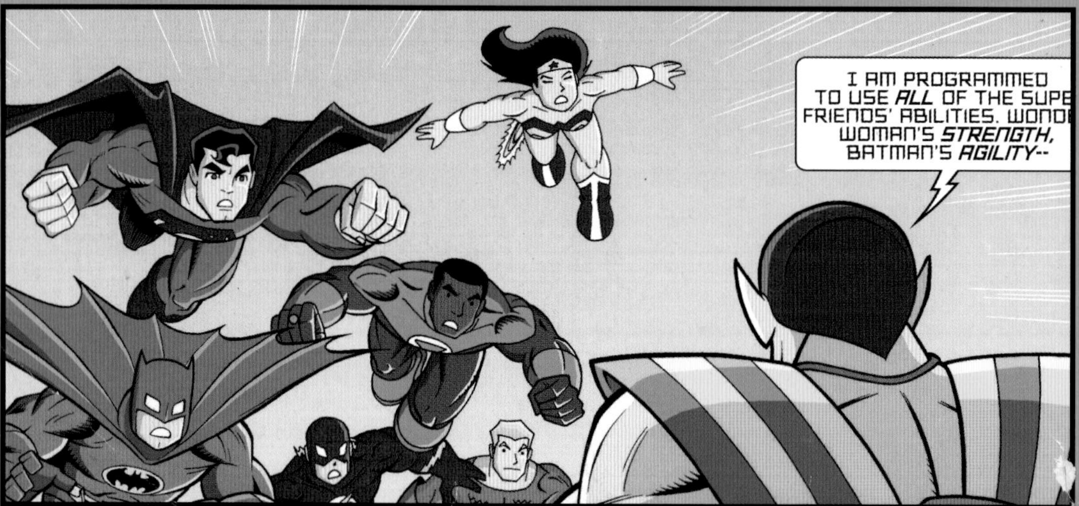
I AM PROGRAMMED TO USE *ALL* OF THE SUPE FRIENDS' ABILITIES. WONDE WOMAN'S *STRENGTH*, BATMAN'S *AGILITY*--

GLOSSARY

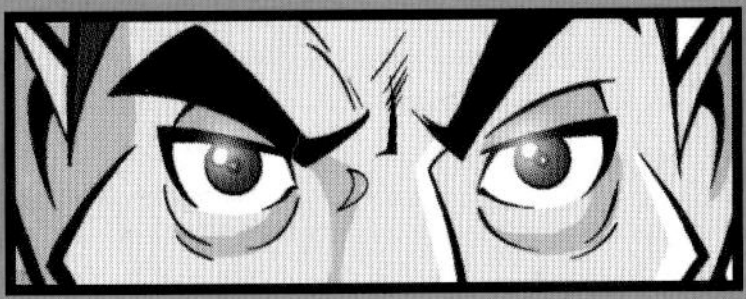

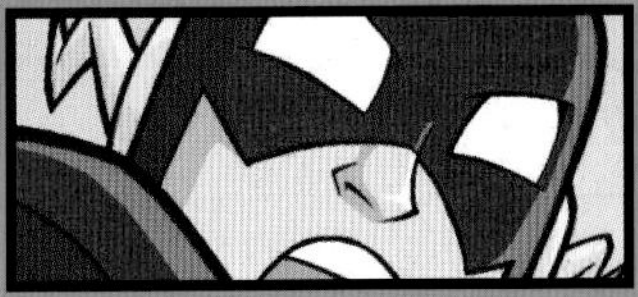

clever [KLEV·er]-smart, witty, or quick in learning

conquer [KON·ker]-to get or gain by force of arms

conqueror [KON·ker·er]-one who conquers

distracted [di·STRAK·tid]-drew the attention or mind to something else, often in order to gain an advantage

empire [EM·pie·er]-a large territory or a number of territories or peoples under one ruler with total authority

entranced [en·TRANSSD]-put into a trance, which is a stupor or sleeplike state

glaciers [GLAY·shurz]-large bodies of ice moving slowly down a slope or valley or spreading outward on a land surface

ice cap [ICE KAP]-a large glacier forming on level land and flowing outward from its center

keelhaul [KEEL·hall]-to haul under the keel of a ship as punishment or torture, or to scold severely

surrender [sir·REN·durr]-to give over to the power, control, or possession of another especially by force

threaten [THRET·en]-to make threats against

useless [YOOSS·less]-having or being of no use

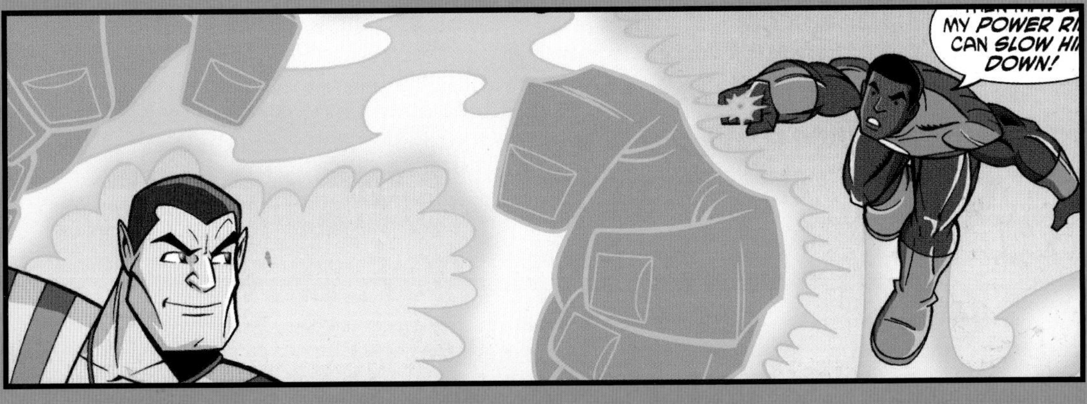
MY POWER
CAN SLOW
DOWN!

VISUAL QUESTIONS & PROMPTS

1. What do the little lines over Aquaman's head mean?

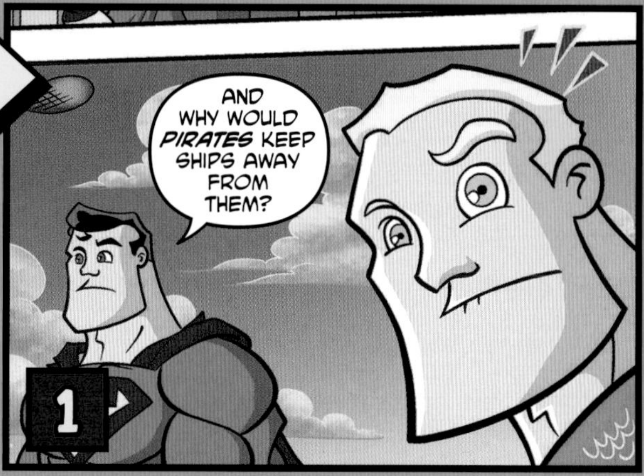
AND WHY WOULD *PIRATES* KEEP SHIPS AWAY FROM THEM?
1

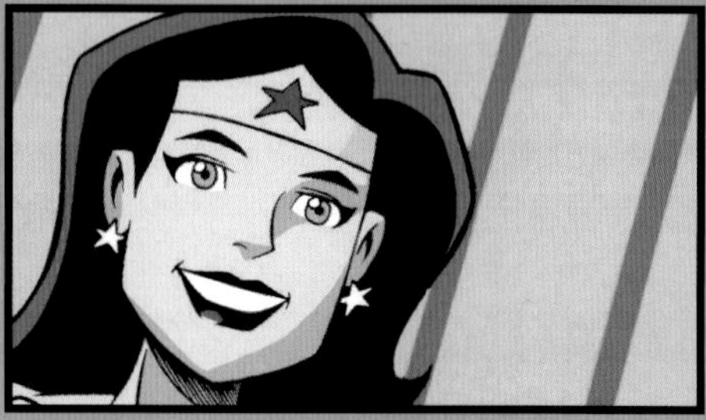

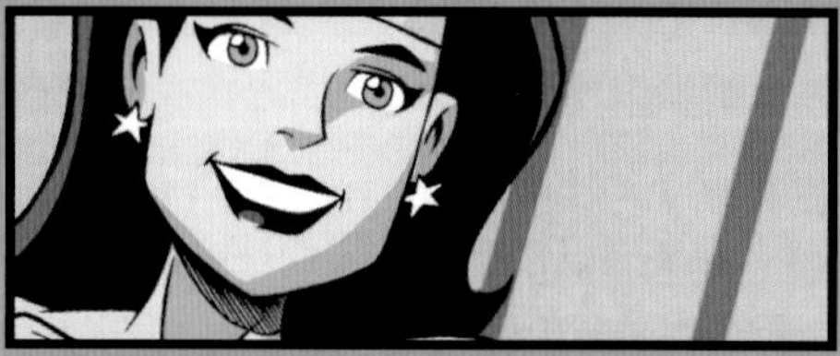

2. Flash loves his pirate hat. Which super hero in this book do you think would be the best pirate? Why?

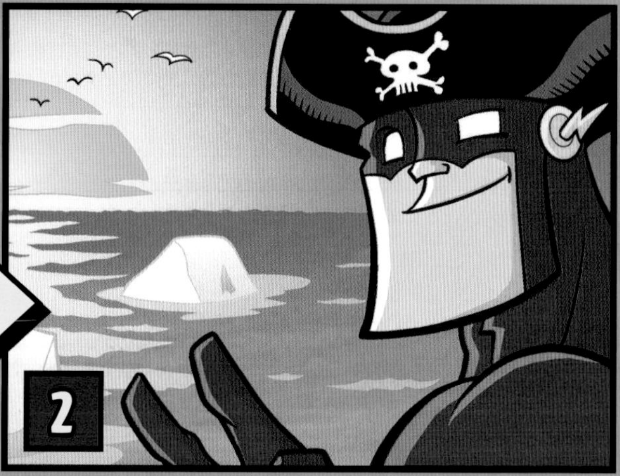
2

3. Green Lantern helps Batman cross the ocean because the Dark Knight can't fly. Identify a few other parts of this book where one hero helps another.

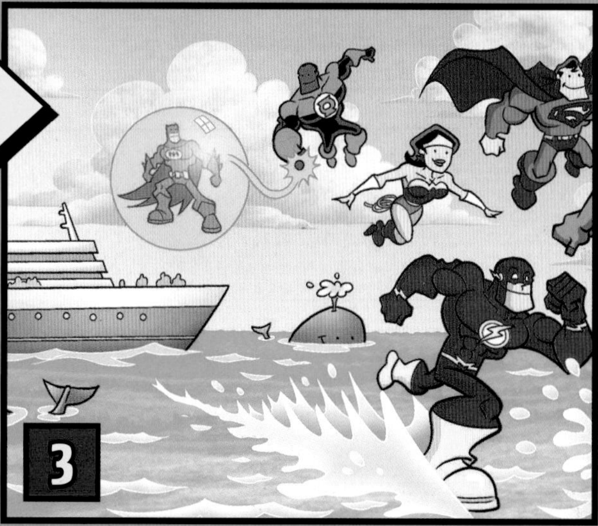
3

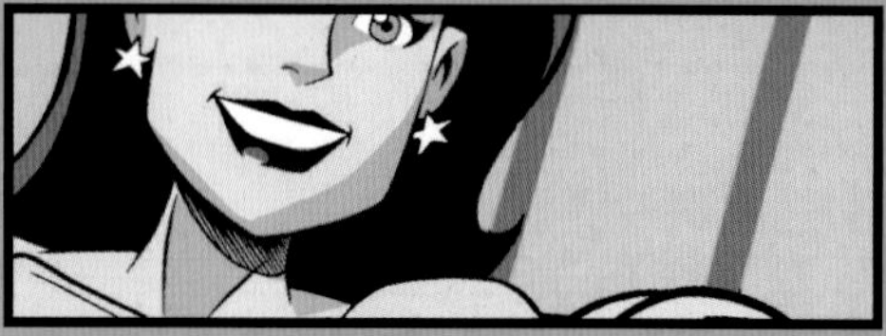

4. Green Lantern used a salt pump to stop Starro. What are some other ways he could have used his powers to stop the seafaring starfish super-villain?

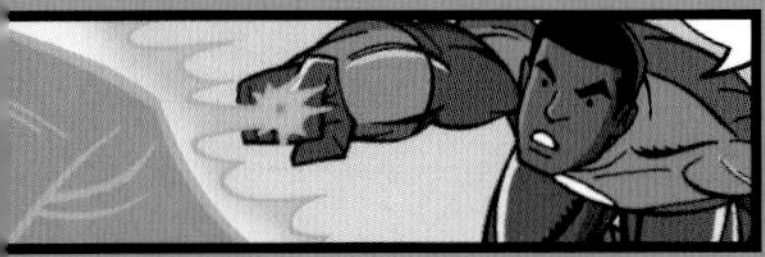

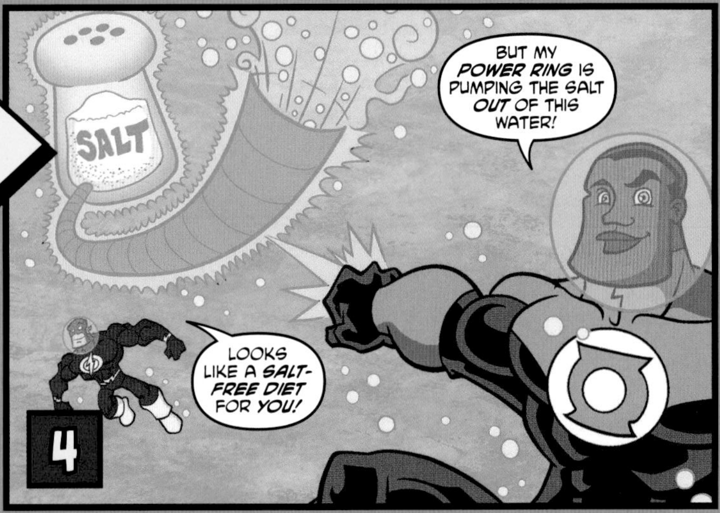
SALT
BUT MY *POWER RING* IS PUMPING THE SALT *OUT* OF THIS WATER!
LOOKS LIKE A *SALT-FREE DIET* FOR *YOU!*
4

5. Take a good look at the first image of Starro that we see. Based on this panel alone, what do you think Starro is like based on how he looks?

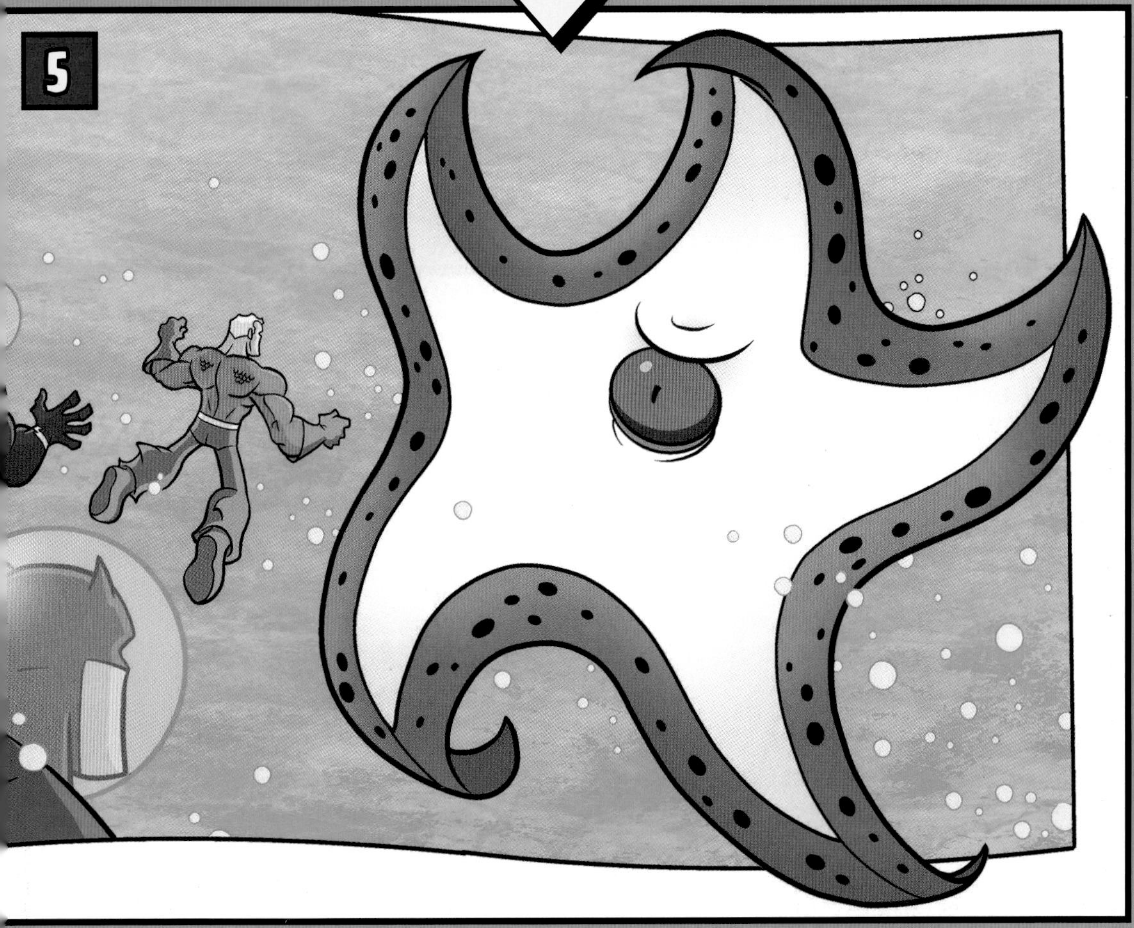
5

READ THEM ALL!

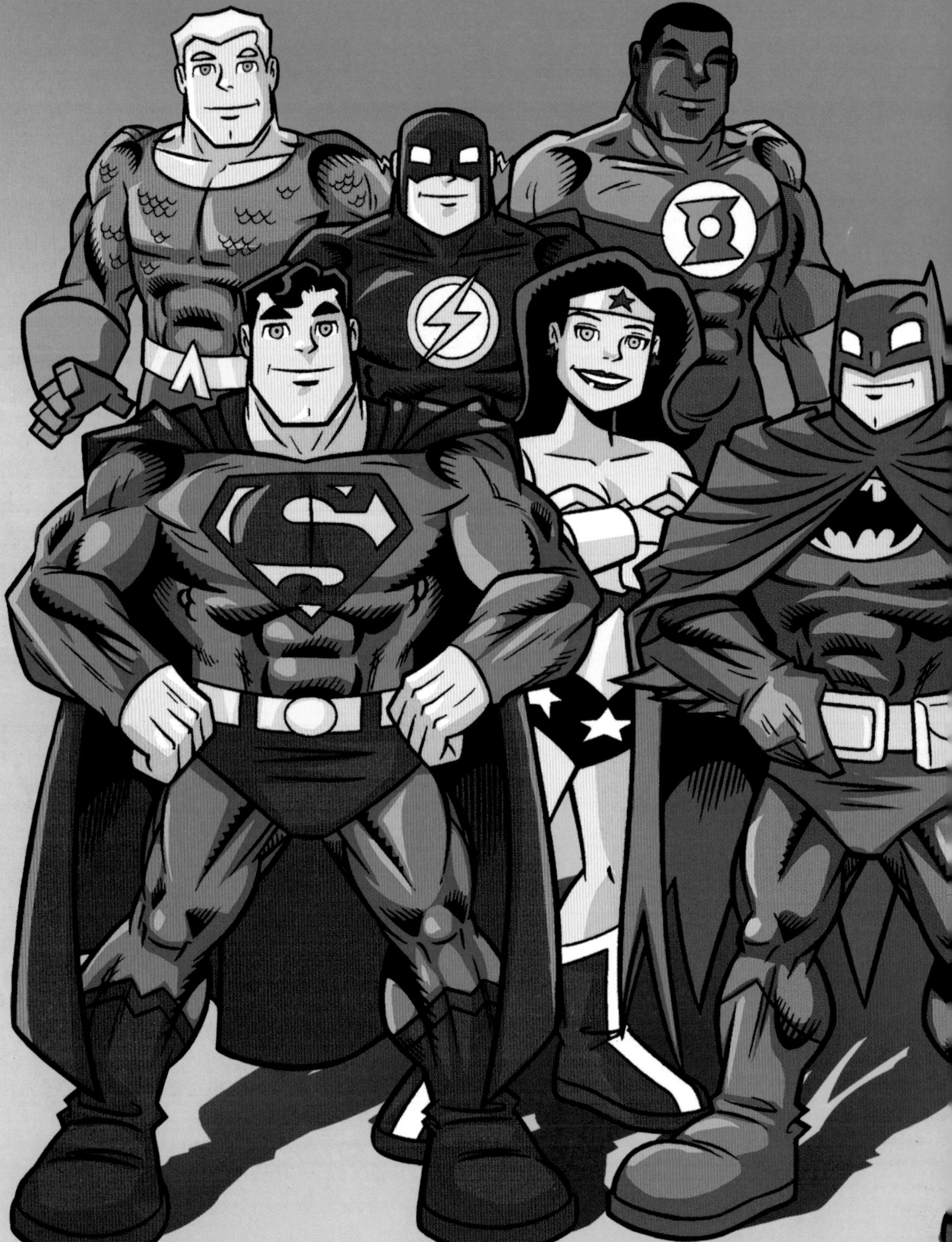

DC SUPER FRIENDS™

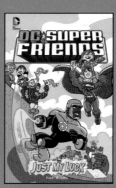

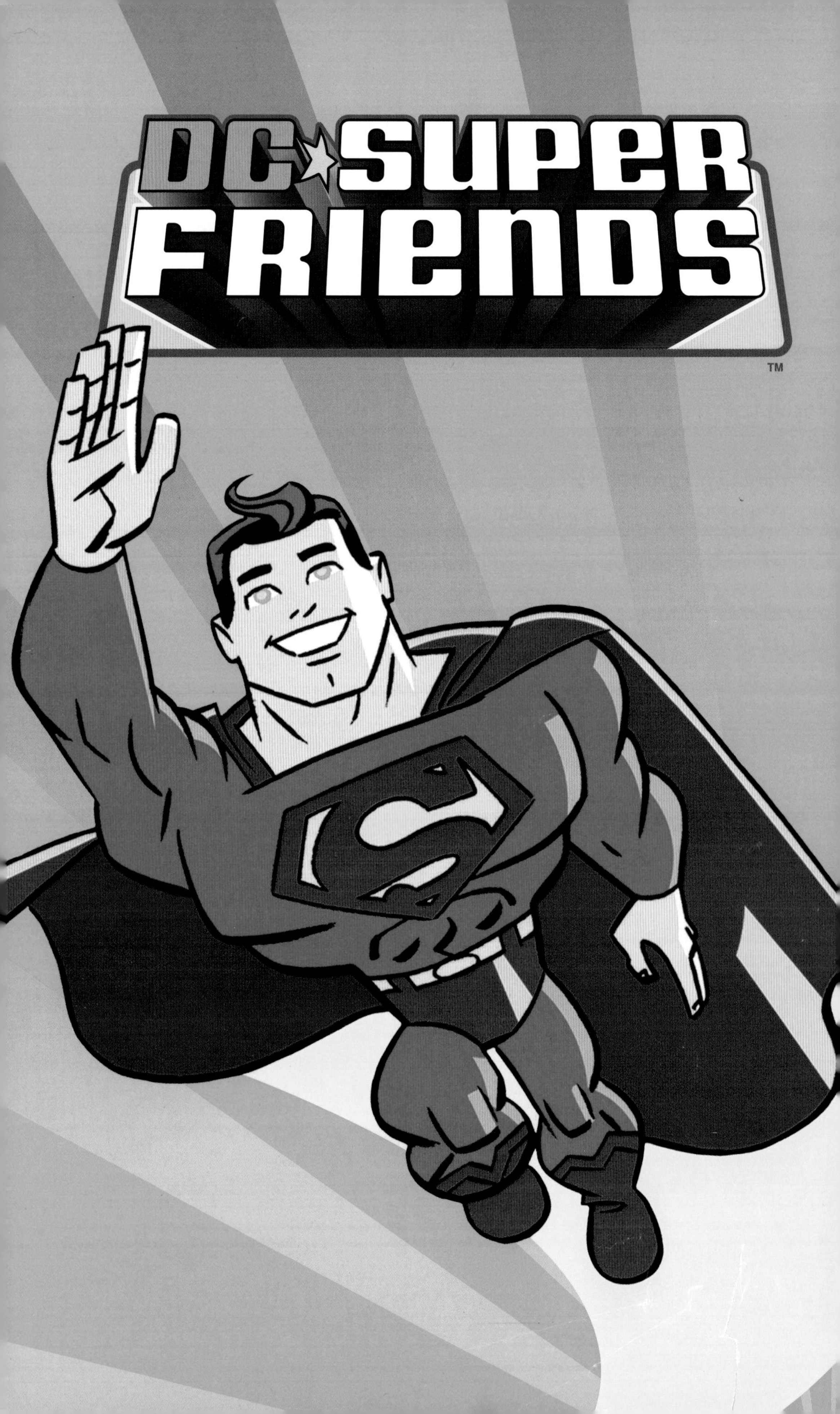
DC SUPER FRIENDS
TM